GOD'S
AUTOBIO

GOD'S AUTOBIO

Stories by

ROLLI

[N₁ [O₂ [N₁
CANADA

Library and Archives Canada Cataloguing in Publication

Rolli, 1980–
God's autobio : stories / by Rolli.

Short stories.
ISBN 978-1-926942-02-5

I. Title.

PS8635.O4465G63 2011   C813'.6   C2011-905914-2

Printed and bound in Canada on 100% recycled paper.

Now Or Never Publishing
#1101, 1003 Pacific Street
Vancouver, British Columbia
Canada V6E 4P2

nonpublishing.com
Fighting Words.

for Trudeau's head

Contents

IMPOSSIBLE FICTIONS

Von Claire and the Tiger

Having never been swallowed by a tiger before, Professor Von Claire wasn't sure what to do about the situation. Strange—whenever one of his colleagues presented him with a dilemma, he could come up with ten solutions on the spot, with plenty of literary allusions, and quotes running gleefully from his pores. It had occurred to him, more than once, that this might be the reason others referred to him as "Tweedmouth," if that *was* the term. It's so easy to mistake what people are saying from the opposite end of a busy cafeteria. *Tweedmouth.* As if one can help being well-read. "Reading maketh a full man," as Bacon said, and surely a full man maketh a better companion than a hollow one. It was a puzzle, to be certain. But there were other things for the professor to wonder about now.

The first thing he'd done, when the tiger had swallowed him, was to feel himself all over, to be sure no pieces were missing. Lucky for him, this tiger never listened to its mother, and swallowed things without chewing them properly. While he was busy thinking of a second thing to do, he realized he was floating on something; what, exactly, he couldn't say. He'd reached down, at one point, to touch the something—and it was so much like a damp spongy tongue that he retracted his arm in an instant. The stomach was, of course, absolutely dark, but the professor held the hope that, if the tiger would only open its mouth a crack, he'd be able to get a better look at his surroundings.

And so he waited, floating in the dark, with his knees drawn up to his chin. Though he wasn't inclined to boredom (his mind was far too active), with no reading material at hand, things were starting to get tedious, if only just a little. For a while, he recited poetry—Blake seemed appropriate—but this was awkward going with a handkerchief over his face (the smell of a tiger's insides is as bad as one could imagine). Besides, he didn't want to offend the beast. Perhaps it preferred Coleridge.

Before too long, Von Claire found himself slipping into a philosophical mindset; he couldn't be blamed, under the circumstances. He thought of Bacon, of Plato, even of Rousseau, which consoled him a little. Still, the situation was dire. It wasn't very likely that he'd survive. It was a wonder that he was still living. As far as deaths go, it wouldn't be an *ignoble* one, really. A pretty rare one, in fact. He was getting on in years. Could have been worse—slumping over a pile of unmarked papers, or withering away, useless and emeritus, on an advisory board or something. His affairs were in order, at least. Ever since a health scare several years back (he'd been struck by a bus), the professor made a point, every six months, to revise his will and burn any incriminating documents. He wouldn't be caught off-guard again. He had no children to leave behind, and very little family. Certainly, his death would have an effect on his peers. Or would it? They'd been increasingly cold towards him. At times, he suspected they might not like him *at all*. Besides the solitary lunches, there was . . . the *limerick*. Something that had circulated through the department a while back, but wasn't meant to fall into his hands. How had it gone?

The aged Professor Von Claire
so firmly holds onto his chair,
that if cries of "curmudgeon!" and "badger!" won't budge him,
we'll just have to pull on his hair
(or what's left of it).

When he'd first read it, he'd thought of raising hell, of taking a bucket up and down the halls to catch the rolling heads, but in the end, once the anger had subsided, did—nothing. Dismissed it as the errant opinion of a prankster (probably Dr. Allen, who taught *pop fiction*, of all the things to teach), and soon forgot about the matter.

A low rumble. The professor wasn't sure if it was a growl, or some intestinal business. Midway through deciding which, the fluid on which he was bobbing began to slosh around, and he had to grip his fingers into the spongy stuff, unpleasant as that was, to keep from falling headlong into it.

He must be active again, the professor thought. *It's been about twenty minutes; I need to sit down for at least that long after a good meal, and have a—the lighter!* Remembering the silver BIC in his jacket pocket. He'd given up smoking some twenty years ago, but still had a cigarette or two after meals, and on his birthday and that kind of thing. The lighter had been a gift from a—well, nothing more than an *admirer*, once upon a time, who had wanted him to give up the habit. There was an inscription to that effect. But over time, his health remaining vigorous, the warning had become easier to ignore. So he kept the habit, and gave up the admirer. Von Claire took the lighter out of his pocket, and flicked it on. In the three or four seconds before it fell, tremblingly, out of his hand, he saw horrors enough to keep a braver man wakeful for the rest of his years.

The cavernous stomach—much larger than he expected it to be—branched out into many smaller chambers. And everywhere—floating in juices, sliding down walls, the remains of the animal's earlier victims, all in various states of decay, a few nothing more than cloth and bone.

To judge by the preponderance of tweed and briefcases, the great animal had a fondness for academics. Floating very close to him was a skull, the flesh entirely eroded, but the glasses of its unfortunate owner still intact thanks to a wet mass of brown hair that held the arms in place. This would have been comical if it weren't so gruesome.

"Grisly, grisly," he muttered to himself, "like the Roman catacombs. Or something out of Poe." He was thankful that it had been such a brief glimpse, and the place was dark again. Holding the handkerchief to his face, he thought frequently of Proverbs, and came very close to vomiting.

An hour passed, perhaps. In that time, he lapsed from a state of high anxiety to one of relative calm—or resignedness, at least. And then, a little psychological magic-trickery. *It all happened so quickly, didn't it? And I was so fearful of what I might see, and the circumstances, and everything, that the whole awful sight was probably just an imaginative quirk. Yes, I'm sure of it. A fantasy. A crock of rubbish!* Droll, the way people do this.

He was mid-way through a sigh of relief, when:

"So?" boomed a voice, sending all the professor's hairs on end. It was the tiger speaking, there was no doubt about it. It's not as if he'd ever heard a tiger speak before—he hadn't thought it possible, even—but the tone of the voice was so low and growly that, well, he just *knew*.

"Cat got your tongue?" said the voice. It seemed to come from all around him, echoing and re-echoing so violently through the various chambers that the professor had to pause a while afterwards, puzzling the sound waves together like a bat, into something sensible.

"Hello?" said the professor, at last, shaking.

"You've made yourself comfortable?" asked the tiger.

"Thank you. Yes," said the professor, not knowing if the beast meant it, or if, god forbid, it had a sense of humour. He wondered how the animal could speak in such an . . . *inward* way, and without admitting any light. *But then, I'm no zoologist,* he thought. *I'll have to ask Dr. Shimmlepinnick.*

"Could I offer you anything to eat?" asked the animal. "Perhaps to drink?"

"No—thank you," said the professor, in as gracious a tone of horror as he could.

"A little more light, maybe?"

"No, no," trembling. "I've always enjoyed darkness. It's—stimulating."

"Good," said the tiger, after one pause, and before another.

"Sir?" asked the professor, in a small voice.

"Beg your pardon?"

"*Sir?*" more distinctly.

"Go ahead."

"I was just wondering if—well, if there was any chance, perhaps, if—well—"

"Yes?"

"If you could be letting me go now—or soon? In the very near future, perhaps?"

"Oh. Hmm. Well. Absolutely not," replied the tiger.

"Ah," crestfallen. And then, "May I ask why not?"

"You may," said the tiger.

A long pause.

"Let's see," said the tiger. "You may not think so, but I'm a fair animal. If you can come up with a good reason *why* I should let you go, unmolested and undigested, I'll let you—happily."

This was the first good news the professor had received in a long while. In the last week alone, his novel idea for attracting new students (by offering an advanced course on Renaissance prose) had been scoffed at by the department heads, and to add insult to injury, Anacreon—his beloved pet of twenty years—had keeled over in his litter box. And now this tiger business. . . .

"Well, there's my career," said the professor, hopefully.

The tiger snorted. "You seriously think the world will miss one more mediocre egghead?"

Von Claire thought of drawing himself up stiffly—would have, too, if there'd been any chance the tiger could have seen the gesture.

"With respect, sir," he said, "I'd hardly call someone who graduated, *with honours*, from Cor—"

"Tell me," interrupted the tiger: "do you really think you're better, or more deserving, or intelligent, even, than anyone who languished in the ivy a few years *less*? And I hope you don't think someone who churns out the occasional paper for some mossy periodical—thousands do—deserves an asterisk by his name."

"You seem to know a lot about me," said the professor, poutily.

"Of course. If you think I just go about randomly stuffing people into my jaws, you're mistaken. I'm not that kind of tiger."

Von Claire shuddered. No—this was an animal of very specific tastes.

"Care to take another shot at it?"

"Hmm?"

"Hurry up, now. I don't have all day."

Von Claire stammered. He never was one to function well under pressure, preferring—not to *dawdle*, as some claimed—but to do a thorough, proper job of everything. His was "a mind that reveres details," as Lewis would say, and that kind of reverence takes time. Whenever necessity forced him to outrun his natural pace, he became jittery, scatter-headed, and struggled to make the simplest decisions.

"You have no children?" asked the tiger, at last.

"No," answered the professor, wringing his hands, but glad the ball was rolling again.

"Friends?"

"Oh, yes. Plenty."

"Except they're more *colleagues* and *associates* than friends in a genuine sense?"

"Well—"

"Come on, now."

Von Claire considered, then answered, "I suppose, yes."

"And they wouldn't *grieve* you, exactly, if you died."

The professor said nothing, but the tiger said, "A few might even be glad of it, eh?"

A long sigh, and quiet.

"Isn't there anyone who depends on you?"

"You would know," said the professor, moodily, then adding, "My cat—up till recently."

"And now?"

No answer.

"I suppose you enjoy your life?" said the tiger.

"Oh, yes," said Von Claire. "Immensely."

"*Immensely*," repeated the beast, stretching out the word like sinew from bone. "And tell me, please, if you'll be so kind, what brings you this—*immense satisfaction*?"

"Well . . . lots of things, I suppose. My research, for instance."

"Your research?"

"Yes. Important stuff—on the nature and function of punctuation from Homer to Hemingway. For a book I hope to publish."

A curious gush of wind (it was the animal sighing). "Anything else?" it asked.

"Lecturing. Reading."

"Walks in the park, and that sort of thing?"

"Very much so. And travel."

"Oh—where do you travel to?"

"To England, mostly. My homeland. You know, 'the throne of kings, the sceptred isle, the earth of majesty, the seat of—'"

"I'm afraid I'm going to have to digest you now."

"What?"

Von Claire nearly passed out. It was only the certainty of a death by drowning in noxious juices that kept him conscious, and clinging to the spongy matter (he never *had* figured out what it was) with ferocity.

"Don't sound so surprised," said the tiger. "You failed to provide a single reason for me *not* to."

"But—"

"Do you have any idea how many people I consume every year?"

No answer.

"More than you could imagine. It's rare that your kind—the bald-pate bachelor—is anything more than leather and bone. A lot of chewing, with very little reward. Sometimes I feel more like a panda gorging itself on bamboo than a tiger."

Von Claire held his stomach.

"Still," said the animal, "it's far less than I used to eat. My former preference was for larger, more *robust* men, a more athletic type. But these men, you see, typically have large, robust families; and no sooner had I eaten the husband than I'd feel badly for the widow; rectify the matter by mercifully gobbling *her* up; then the children, grandparents, cousins, etc., following a similar logic. And going around eating entire villages is, you can imagine, exhaustive, not to mention, to my mind, immoral. I am, sir, above all, a tiger with a conscience. I made some permanent changes to my diet, and now eat selectively, with the fussiness of a house cat, only those who can't possibly matter to anyone."

"Why didn't you just kill me on the spot?" said the professor, miserably.

"Because it didn't *happen* that way," said the tiger, gently. "I'll bet when you eat—peas, say—that, now and then, one goes down whole. Well, swallowing a *whole one* gives *me* a unique opportunity: to learn more about my prey."

"And what have you learned?" asked the professor. There was anger and sadness in his voice—though strange to say, part of him admired the beast. It had, like himself, an inquiring (if cruel) spirit. A curious animal, at the very least.

"I haven't finished my examination," said the tiger, in a smiling way. "Or have you given up?"

"Absolutely not," said Von Claire, horrified.

"Good. We'll continue. Let's see . . . you've sacrificed the pleasures of love, family, friendship, for what reason? Those articles? Your little book, or something; something to do with punctuation or other?"

"*The Nature and Function of Punctuation from Homer to Hemingway,*" Von Claire repeated, in one breath. "I feel there's a distinct *need* for such a volume at this time. It's a branch of research that's been cruelly neglected."

"Sounds like a lot of work."

"Can you blame a man for being ambitious?"

"No. Though I can, perhaps, for being deluded, deceitful, and ignorant in the extreme."

"Slander," said the professor, surprised at his daring, "is something I will *not* tolerate."

A low chuckle.

"It's like this, fellow," said the tiger. "There are, I've discovered, little flourishes of wealth and status that give some of your kind an edge in life. But the bulk of people are on the same footing. Now and then—not so often as you might think—one of them decides he's either better, or wants to be better than the rest. This same person would, if he could (the desire is insatiable), have the whole world kneeling at his feet—like Ramses, or something. You're familiar with Ramses?"

"Naturally," said the professor, insulted. "*All* of the Ramses."

"Good for you. I once swallowed an Egyptologist. He was a good conversationalist—for a time. Where was I? Right—the name given to this starving desire, this grossest form of vanity imaginable, is *ambition*."

"I hardly want the world at my feet. I hardly expect it—despite the importance of my work."

"But you'd take it if you got it?" said the tiger.

"Well—"

"And if you didn't, well, the adulation might always come posthumously."

Von Claire thought a while, then said, "That *does* happen on occasion, yes. I think each generation is a little wiser than the last."

"But never wise enough to catch the importance of things the first time around, eh?"

The professor was about to retort when a sudden, swirling draft of air (it was the animal yawning) sent the unpleasant lump of stuff on which he was floating into such a twirl that his glasses flew off his face and splashed into the acidic mixture below. He was disheartened, at first—glasses are a precious thing to any far-sighted academic—but had no trouble consoling himself. It was too dark to read, even if the right materials were available. And he was always being told his horn-rims were ugly and old-fashioned, anyway.

A second gust, and then—

"If you can't think of a single reason why I should spare you," said the tiger, "you're an even duller fellow than I imagined."

"Charity," said a small voice.

"Beg your pardon?"

"*Charity*," repeated the professor, with more confidence. "Unlike, I'm sure, most of my colleagues, I give upwards of five percent of my income to a number of charitable concerns."

"Why?"

Von Claire was taken aback, but went on, stutteringly, "Wa—well for a, for the sake of doing good, of course."

"You're a selfless man?"

"I'd like to think so, yes."

"Or a self-satisfied?"

"You're a very cynical animal."

"In search of water," snarled the tiger, "is it cynical to avoid the desert? The world's a pretty miserable place, and your petty contributions, and the pooled contributions of a million other petty sources, won't rectify that; they amount to squat. The only real effect charity can have is on oneself. From what I've gathered, you people feel good when you help others, you derive pleasure from it. I'm surprised more people don't approach charity the way they do sex, and give a little something to the poor every Friday night. If it was painful to help others, on the other hand, if doing so produced a sensation like that of electric shock, and people *still* emptied their pockets—well, *that* would be selfless, *that* would be charity. The rich know how unfair their position is—and the only way they can assuage their guilt, and sleep at night, is through little grains of charity, taken like a sedative. I once swallowed a preacher who was both the happiest and most despicable creature I've ever encountered. Now, there's nothing wrong with generosity in itself, but delusion is a dangerous vice."

"You do this to torment me," said the professor. "A sick game. Anacreon wouldn't just eat a mouse outright; he'd torture it for hours."

"All in the interest of science. As I said, these interviews afford me an opportunity to find out more about my prey. With you, for instance . . ." fishing for a "what" or some other reply. When it was clear one wasn't forthcoming, the beast went on, "I found—a *confirmation*." The fish came this time, and the tiger, grasping it, replied, "A confirmation that you're just as worthless as I imagined you'd be, and it's high time I finished you off."

"But what if," said Von Claire, feebly, and frantic, "what if I promised to *change*."

"Hmm?" said the tiger, in an amused tone.

"I'd like to think I could . . . *improve* myself, in various ways. Whatever you suggest. *Anything*."

"Sir, that's a delightful idea," said the tiger, warmly. "A perfect solution. I congratulate you."

The professor sighed, sweating and relieved.

"Then you'll let me go?" he asked.

"Of course not," said the tiger. "If you were thirty or forty years younger, maybe. It is, of course, by this point, far too late."

A whimper in the dark.

"Don't be a child about it, now."

But Professor Von Claire went on sobbing. The tiger waited for him to finish—it took ten or fifteen minutes, at least—and then, in a slow whisper, said:

"There *isn't* any reason, is there, why I shouldn't kill you on the spot?"

A drawn-out silence . . .

And a *very* brief scream.

"For supper," said the tiger, "I think I'll have . . . a poet."

THE SPLENDID NEW CRACK

So an angel comes from wherever and says to me, "Hey. *Hey.* I'll give you anything you want. Any one thing. Think hard. But be quick about it," smoking a cigarette.

Well, I thought about it. Quick and hard. And I said, "I wanna splendid new crack."

Consider it. Pissing, shitting. It's elimination, right, it's vital? But more than that, it's *pleasurable.* Admit it. The relief you feel, after pissing or shitting. Like chocolate. Sex. Better, than sex. It lasts longer.

More holes is more pleasure. A new crack is a new reason to smile. To get up, in the morning. Yeah.

So he hoofs out the cigarette, the angel, says, "Whatever floats your boat." Snaps his fingers.

And there it was.

Right—in the middle—of my forehead.

It was awesome.

So I went for a walk. Showing off. Man, you should've seen the looks on their faces. When they saw it. My splendid new crack. It was like . . . serious, serious envy. Wanting what you've got, so bad. I could've strutted around all day. All the fucking day. But there was only one place I wanted to go. One person, I wanted to see.

So there was this chick, at the coffee shop, Daily Grind, 'round the corner. This waitress. Had the hots for her, *years.* I fucking *ached* for this girl, man. Burned. She never seemed interested, though. But it's a matter of confidence, right? I never had the right—confidence.

Well, you should've seen me, now. Waltzed right into the place. Grinning. Confident. Feeling, like, as good as a man can fucking possibly feel. Solid—gold.

So I sit down. Waiting. Watching her working. Her ass. *Man.*

So she finally comes over.

"What'll it be?" she says, not really looking at me, tapping her pad on the tabletop, checking out some bearded dude at the door.

"Coffee," I say, deliberately. Cuz I knew it would get her attention. In a place like that, asking for coffee is like . . . asking for a kiss. In a brothel. So she turns, and she glares at me.

And she sees it. I can tell she sees it, cuz—she looks away. Tries too hard to look at everything *else*, you know? Like when a cripple limps by.

"Sorry," she says. "You wanted . . . coffee?"

"Just coffee," I say.

Getting a peek in, now and then, slyly, "Not . . . flavoured?" she says.

I shake my head. I shake my head and smile.

"What, um . . . roast, would you like?" She looks again, real quick. Not quick enough.

"Whatever," I say.

"Medium fine?" she asks.

"Sure, sure," I say, grinning, leaning back.

"*Are you taking a shit*?" she says, her jaw falling.

Cuz that's what was happening. When I'm nervous, my bowels . . . try and move. So I've gotta clench up. I was clenched up down there, all right. But . . . not up above. Trying to act cool, and everything. It just . . . slips out. Slips out, lands right in the middle of the table.

"Oh my *god*," she says, dropping her pad. Her pen. "What the fuck is *wrong* with you?"

And this gets people interested. A couple guys push their chairs back, rush up, thinking maybe I've groped her or something, and if they seem all manly and heroic maybe they'll get the same chance later. By invite.

Somebody shouts. People are . . . all around me. Groaning. *Gagging*. Laughing and throwing up.

"What a shithead," says some guy. Some asshole, who thinks he's clever.

So I—I'm in a panic. And that does not help the shit situation, I'll tell you. It was just . . . pouring down my face. Off my chin. All the shit over. Fuck.

So I push through the crowd. People are screaming. Leaping back. But in a second, I'm out the door. I'm gone.

When I get back home, my apartment, I sit in front of the mirror, the bathroom. Clean up. I wasn't . . . so sure about the crack anymore. But it was a part of me. We live with the decisions we make. I don't think . . . I regret it, not exactly. But.

So basically I'm an outcast. Like a hunchback or something. In a sanctuary. It's—pretty lonely. Yeah.

In the daytime, I stay in. Sleep, mostly. Read. At night . . . I'm out there. Rattling trash cans. Scrounging for food. I think I've become an urban legend.

Most urban legends are true.

But you know, I'm just like everybody else. I am just like *everybody* else. I've got a secret.

So do you.

The Irrepressible Head
of Pierre Elliott Trudeau

The summer turned to fog. I hate when that happens. Waiting all the long winter for things to heat up a bit, and when they finally do. . . . Like being stuck in a bathroom. Nothing but a big dull novel to read. Fog's alright to look at. Not to step out into. Like a cat that way. In the wintertime, you know? Just looking out the window. Looking and waiting.

And then there was Trudeau. Fifteenth Prime Minister of Canada. His head. His *bust*. Bought it at a rummage years back. Brought it with me to London. To remind me of my home and native land. Never much cared for Trudeau. Politics. Nice bust, though, like bronze, but not. And hollow. Had "Trudeau" spelled out on the front of it. Or I wouldn't've guessed. But it had character. Aquiline, I think the word is. Awfully aquiline. And cheap. A buck. Put it on my bookshelf. Forgot about it pretty quick. Stuff to do.

Had the thing for two years, I think, when it happened. I'd just got home. Worked late. Threw my coat onto the coat rack. Hung up my umbrella. Hate the rain, personally. Almost as bad as the fog. There's no sun in this country.

All of a sudden—it's like people say, the hairs on their neck— I was bristling. There was a voice—of someone. I live alone. I live alone, and there was a voice. I couldn't make it out. It was . . . coming from my study.

I stepped forward. Slowly. Thought of going back for the umbrella, or a ball bat if I had one. But something about the voice (couldn't make out what it was saying, just yet). It was eerie, sure. But not *threatening*. So I moved forward, unarmed. Slowly. Very much like a cat. Into the hall.

There was a light on in the study. The light spilled out into the dark hall. I hadn't left it on, I was sure. I moved closer to the doorway. The voice grew louder. I could make out bits of it, now. . . .

". . . as Voltaire said. As he *would* say now, I'm sure. If he were living."

"Or was it Rousseau?"

"It *was* Rousseau."

Very close, now. I looked for a shadow. In the doorway. Waiting. Listening.

"Though it might've been Diderot."

I grabbed hold of the frame of the door. And leaned in slowly.

"Oh, hello."

I glanced around.

"Hello, I said."

I was dumbfounded.

"Well?"

The room was empty. I checked under the desk. The closet. Out the window.

"*Well?*" said the voice, again.

And then I understood.

It was Trudeau.

The head.

The bust.

Talking.

"A handshake would be a good place to start."

His voice—its voice—was . . . exactly like Trudeau's. Like, slow and lackadaisical. Like you know your shit. Sure of it. Even when you're full of it.

"What the fuck are you waiting for?"

The lips . . . didn't move. When it spoke. But the sound came from inside. It seemed. I thought.

Walked over to the bookshelf. Picked up the bust. Gave it a good shake.

"I said *handshake*," snapped the PM. "Would *you* like to have your brains rattled?"

"But . . . you didn't talk *before*," was all I could say. I felt drunk. I cannot state enough that I don't drink. Except on occasion.

"*That,* naturally," said Trudeau, as if the answer were embossed on his forehead, "is because I was studying the French philosophers."

I wondered how he managed that. But didn't ask.

"Monsieur, monsieur, you have wasted your life. *I* should know. I've watched it happen. I've sat here and watched, with the patience of a—French philosopher. *Gaspillé, gaspillé.* Have you ever even *read* Mounier?"

Had to confess I hadn't even heard of him.

"Have you ever even *drunk* Sauternes?"

I was—wasn't sure if he was being metaphorical.

"I am not the Ghost of Christmas Past, monsieur. You will not be redeemed, like a coupon from the Sunday gazette. *C'est terminé.*"

"Why?" I said. This was after . . . a long waiting.

He whispered. If he could've leaned in . . . he would've. I'm sure.

"Because I said so."

"Oh."

Could've said more. Been witty, or something. But the room was pretty bright. Brighter than before, I thought. I could only think—of the brightness. Holding up my hand.

There was a pair of sunglasses on the bookshelf. I'd left them there. So I slipped them on. That was better.

"I'll be having a little soiree, this evening."

I nodded.

"You'll wait outside. Till morning."

"It's raining," I said.

"So it is."

I turned to leave.

"One more thing," said Trudeau.

I turned again.

"Your soup is incomestible, at best."

And here I am. Out in the cold. The rain. Feeling displaced, sort of. You know? I sit . . . where the light spills out. The bay window. Looking in. Who's coming and going. It's—it takes some getting used to. But I've seen three celebrities so far. Beau Bridges. Liz Taylor, wheeled in by a big guy, grey hair, all bones. The other is a princess. I'm pretty sure.

I can't wait to see who shows up next.

FAMILY CRYPT

"Harold?"

"Hmm? What?"

"I've been thinking."

"Oh yeah."

"About—Harold, are you listening?"

"Mmm hmm, mmm hmm."

"Sometimes I wonder. I do, Harold. And I've been thinking."

"You've been thinking, yes."

"And there's something—well there's something I have to say."

"Oh yeah."

"I'm not sure how to say this."

"Right, right."

"It's difficult."

"Difficult. You're right."

"Harold, listen to me."

"Mmm hmm, mmm hmm."

"I'd like. I'd—I'm not sure how to put this, Harold."

"Right."

"I'd like—Harold. Harold, I'd like a . . . a separation."

"Right, right."

"I've been thinking. I mean I've thought it over, for a long time. A very long time, Harold."

"I sure do."

"A very long time now. And Harold, it's over."

"Over on the shelf, yes."

"I'm not sure exactly when it happened. But waking up one day, there it was."

"The top shelf."

"It was simply a—more a building up of—of everything. It wasn't sudden. It wasn't."

"The bottom shelf, try."

"I'm unhappy. I've been unhappy, now, for a long time."

"Someone there?"

"We were in love."

"Someone at the door?"

"Harold, do you remember the night? The first night? It was . . . fifty years ago. In the spring. The rain. The storm shook the blossoms, every one, from the trees."

"Time's it?"

"We walked on blossoms. . . . The smell, Harold."

"Wonderful, wonderful."

"Harold?"

"Wonderful joke."

"Harold."

"Tell it to the boys, tomorrow. Wonderful."

"There were good years, Harold. Many good years. But . . . it's over now."

"Mmm hmm."

"Harold."

"Right, right."

"Over, Harold."

"Yup."

"I'll miss you, Harold. I will."

"Right."

"Harold."

"Time's it?"

"This isn't easy."

"Of course, of course."

"This isn't easy, Harold."

"Six o'clock yet?"

"But I'm not sure. . . . Where will I go?"

"That the TV?"

"Harold, I'm not sure."

"Right, right."

"It's difficult."

"Come again?"

"There's nothing. To say, Harold."

"Mmm hmm."

"Except—Harold, will you . . . will you remember me?"

"Good point."

"Harold?"

"Oh, yeah."

"Will you remember?"

"Right, right."

"It's just I'm not sure."

"Yup."

"I think—I'm not sure, Harold. I'm just not sure anymore."

"Say that again?"

"I'm just—I'm not . . . sure."

"Where is it?"

"It's difficult."

"Good, good."

"It's difficult, Harold. Harold, it is."

"Come again?"

"I don't think—well maybe. Maybe I won't. If it isn't . . . Harold."

"Mmm hmm."

"I'm just—I'm . . ."

"What is it?"

"Harold."

"You say something?"

"I . . ."

"Someone say something?"

"No, Harold, I . . . Harold, no."

"Someone at the door?"

GOD'S AUTOBIO

I'd always thought of God as an Englishman; so when my theory proved true I was, if not surprised, exactly, certainly tickled. Not sure why I ever *made* the assumption. Just did. Suppose I've always been an independent thinker. Others are happy to believe what they're told, to take the cracker and go on parroting nonsense the rest of their lives. But I've always preferred to believe what's *true* according to my own gut—my natural instinct, you know? As a method of plowing through a world full of hypocritical nonsense, it hasn't let me down to date.

We met, God and I, in September of last year. I'd seen him coming, out of the corner of my eye, from a good way off—not God, but a grey sedan piloted by some middle-aged soft-head. Of course, I assumed he'd *stop*. But he was one of those people, not too different from the ones I mentioned above, who's so orthodox—I was jaywalking, technically—that he'd've thought nothing of crushing my skeletal system just because he had the right of way. Which is just what he did. You can forgive me, my memory, for being a little patchy after that. There were sirens, and hands. A bright room. A scrap of conversation:

"It's difficult."

"Yes. A difficult profession. And hard to tell—you run through so many people in a day—when you're doing a good job of it. But I flip through the obituaries in the evening, and if I don't see any of my patients, I take a shot of whiskey."

"And if you do?"

"I take two."

Though I was aware of more talk, and movement, both became softer and far-off; *I* became softer and far-off *feeling*, all floaty and light-headed. I went out of my body, above the hospital bed, into a tunnel of light (the same old story). The tunnel grew both brighter and narrower as I went, ending in a round brilliance no bigger than my head. I reached out, the light swelled, and then—darkness.

It was temporary, thank God (though for a while I wondered if I'd gone "direct the other way"). A gradual brightening, and I found myself at one end of a dim, narrow—I hesitate to call it a hallway, because it served the purpose of a room. There were no doors or windows that I could see. Loads of bookcases and shelves. A few stands and bric-a-bracs, but nothing too interesting. At the opposite end of the room was a heavy wooden desk, with a lamp on it (the only source of light). And suddenly, with no idea of exactly how I'd gotten there, I was sitting in a plush leather chair in front of the desk. And behind it—the Big Man himself.

I call him the Big Man despite the fact that, at that point, I didn't know for sure whether he was God or not; plus, he was a man of only slightly more than middle height. Well made, lean, clean-shaven. Nothing overtly English about him—no *teeth*— except that he was drinking tea, and smelled strongly of bergamot. He didn't offer me any tea, but I was too stupefied, at the time, to take offense at it. I was busy, besides, trying to catch the titles of some of the books on the shelves around me—you know, not wanting to miss out on the chance, but not wanting to look rude, either, by being too obvious about it. Didn't recognize any of them, though, and only one sticks out in my memory: *The Art of Silhouette*. Droll.

It wouldn't've been courteous to've been the first one to speak. He was in mid-sip, besides. So I waited. He lowered the teacup, savoring the taste as only a true Englishman can. Finally, placidly, he clasped his hands together and began.

"You are?" Such a warm, elegant, absolutely English voice.

"Marino, Bill," I said nervously, on the off chance that his mind was constructed like a vast filing cabinet.

"Mmm hmm." He looked me in the eye, lingeringly—which I'll admit, unnerved me more than a little. So I was relieved when he turned his gaze towards the ceiling—it was a very high one— in a sort of reverie. For a while I wondered if he'd put a bit of something in his tea; but then he looked back at me and said, "If you like, I'll tell you a story."

What could I do but nod, nervous, eager, honored at the privilege. He leaned back in his chair, slipping into a reposed, conversational expression. If he'd had a cigar, I'm sure he'd have smoked it.

"My first, most vivid memory," he said, "was of rising through a substance very like vanilla pudding, or raw yolk, but brightly lit throughout. At first, I could barely distinguish myself from the medium in which I traveled; but it seemed that, the higher I rose, the more *individual* I felt, and the more solid. This impression," pausing for tea, "was confirmed by what I saw around me—frail skeletal forms, by the dozens, materializing; thickening, growing; beginning to move. As I waved my hand before my face, admiring its shape, I noticed a—well, a *scum* for lack of a better word— of white overhead, intensely bright. The fear of passing into this scum—inevitable, since it extended in all directions—was my first strong emotion, first . . . trauma."

He took another sip. I know it was just tea, and I'm not even a tea drinker, but the fact that he went on drinking it in front of me and never offering me any grew more offensive by the minute. When he ran through one cup, he'd pour out another from an inexhaustible pot by his elbow. It was annoying, and drew my focus, from time to time, from what he was saying.

"The others around me must have had similar anxieties, for in the moments before we entered the white—*stratum* (a better word)—there was no end of anticipatory twitching and flailing on their part, like kittens being lowered into a bucket. I suppose we, too, feared drowning, or at the very least the unfamiliar.

"But there was nothing terrible about this whiteness, not in itself. It was thinner, and oily; and I suppose that was why it had risen to the top of this—pool or ocean, I wasn't sure. The real terror came a moment later, when I surfaced. An awful thing, to go from one strange world to another, with no idea what's happening or why. You'll understand me: it's how every member of your race comes into the world," sipping, "and leaves it, too."

I assumed, here, that he meant the human race generally, not Italian Americans.

"There I was—we all were—in a broad patch of sand, bordered by thistles and greenery, suffering not only from the strange newness of our situation, but the dry heat and the wind. I looked at the others closely, now—to know myself. They were like tiny men, slightly more than a foot in height, but with no meat or skin on their bodies, just a delicate, living bonework. I suppose a dozen of them died almost on the spot. The rest of us—some six or seven, at most—instinctively, and fearfully, crawled behind rocks (boulders, to us) or simply stood there, stupefied and shaking."

He refilled his teacup, and took it into his hands, looking at me as if he expected me to say something. So I did—the first thing that came to mind:

"If it had come from anyone else," I said, smiling, "I wouldn't have believed a word of it." We both had a good laugh, mine shrill and nervous, his the rich and mellow laughter of the true Briton.

"Would you like me to keep going?" he asked.

"Of course."

"Good," stirring in his cream and sugar—such an awful lot of sugar. "Shall I flash forward several million years, or leap headlong into philosophical speculations?"

I'd've preferred he picked up where he left off, but that wasn't one of the options. I've never cared much for philosophical speculations, especially other people's, though of course I made an exception here. I could tell from his enthusiasm, and the emphasis he placed on the second option, besides, that he wanted me to pick it.

"Oh, the speculations, please," I said, hoping that they might be interesting after all, or at the very least that his abilities stopped short of the telepathic.

He smiled, and stirred the tea.

"Like you, I'm sure, I've developed my own ideas about life and the universe. I'll make it clear from the beginning that they're theories, only. The truth might be a long way off. Existing as long as I have, though, and having routes to test them in countless ways, they must be, at the very least, half-correct. And there's always a chance I might just be right on the button, too," with that wistful English grin. "To start, then: I am, as far as I can gather, God."

A thrilling tingle down my spine. I'd suspected as much, of course, but to have it confirmed, and him sitting right across from me . . .

"I'm the creator and destroyer, the giver of life, shaper of clay—whatever you care to call me." Adding another sugar lump, "But this wasn't always the case. I've always said, 'Some are born great, some achieve greatness, and some have greatness thrust upon them.'"

"It was *Shakespeare*, actually," I timidly interrupted. Presumptuous, but it had to be said.

"Shakespeare," he said, with a sudden, dark severity, "is only one facet of my divine personality. If you were to throw a ball through someone's window, you couldn't say 'The ball broke it.' *You* broke it. And *I* said it."

Turtle-like, I shrank back into my chair. Clearly, he was the wrong entity to offend. I decided to hold my tongue for a while, after that. He took a few forceful swallows of tea, a deep breath, and, thankfully, mellowed back into his former repose.

"Attaining omnipresence," he went on, "was a long climb up the ladder. How long it took, I can't really say (after the million-year mark, I lost count)." He refilled his cup, and stared wistfully at the ceiling. Finally, "People are always surprised to learn that gods, too, are born and die; but it happens every day. Again, from what I can gather, from what I've experienced—observed—the moment a god is believed in, he (or she, which is often the case), comes into existence, enters the living world. Develops, first, in the fetal liquids I described earlier (though where this fluid exists, geographically, I've never been able to tell), then sets out, motherless and alone.

"Thought is a powerful force. Should any one idea become strong enough, be held by enough people, it *will*—I'm sure of this—influence the world around it and become a physical reality. Let's say a group of people, agricultural types, starts getting edgy about its crops. They might, naturally enough, uncomfortable with having no actual control over the atmosphere, dream up a rain god. And the strength of their sentiment, combining and growing, and existing as a real force, somehow fathers forth such a figure, which will only grow and flourish and become more powerful the more it's believed in. If it's a wise deity, it will do what it can to please its followers. Belief, after all, is its only food. And if it can't—there may be competition from other, similar divines, or it may be too feeble to influence the atmosphere as needed—well, then it withers, expires. Humanity is fickle—vengeful, even—and if one god fails to please it, will swiftly move on to another. And when a god loses believers, faith alone sustaining him, he withers. Goes down, in the end, with his ship, if he can't find any preservers."

I gave a slight chuckle, if only because I thought it was expected. He grinned (who *doesn't* like to think he's funny), and continued:

"During the early years of my life—I speak of millennia, of millions of years, even—I never once encountered a human being—for the simple reason that there were, at that point, none to observe. Plenty of apes, however. I enjoyed watching them, their daily activities of food-gathering and play. And every dawn, when they whooped and hooted at the sun, I felt a curious thrill. It was a long time before I discovered why, exactly. I remember that eureka moment well. I was on a hilltop, lying in the grass, cloud-watching. The temperature had been mild up to that point, but now the sun was directly overhead—too bright and too hot for my liking. I wished it were less so—and it became less so, on both accounts. *A coincidence*, I thought. On a lark, though, I wished it a little warmer—and again, it was. I sat up excitedly, and wondered what that heavenly body would look like *green*. It *changed*, and I was thrilled. The sun was my plaything, after that. I stretched it and folded it, putty-like, into every possible shape, according to my whim.

"The apes, however, were less than thrilled, shrieking at almost every change. Now and then, however, they showed signs of—tolerance, first, then approval, in response to certain changes of brightness, heat, and color. When I became bored of pleasing myself, I set about pleasing *them,* and by experimentation discovered a temperature and size that satisfied the entire group. And the more satisfied they became, the more worshipful, the stronger I felt. I swelled, doubled and redoubled in size. It was clear to me at last. 'I am,' I said to myself, 'a sun-god.' In a long life, that early discovery was, I think, my purest moment of joy." Shutting his eyes to slivers, "I bet I know what you're thinking."

I swallowed, hoping he didn't.

"You're wondering about the others."

"Oh, yes," I said. "Very much. The others."

"The others," he said, "who emerged from the pool," looking up at the ceiling, "the other small gods," *(ah),* "died, for the most part, on the spot. A *few* survived. On occasion, I saw them, usually clinging nervously to one another, like a bunch of possums. I never had any desire for their company, was happy with my independence. They were harmless enough, besides—to a point. But in time, they too grew in size and power, discovered their *congregation.* The one, I remember, was a rain god; the other . . . I don't recollect. But the first was trouble enough. You can imagine *my* frustration, trying to keep things warm and sunny, with a rain god perpetually clouding things over. It soon became necessary, for my sake," sipping, "to intervene. So while he was sleeping (gods *do* sleep), I . . . stopped his breath."

He paused here, as if he expected a remark. But I couldn't think of anything. I mean, what does a person say after that?

"And when the *other* became a problem," he went on, "well, I intervened there as well. It's something I've had to do countless times. It might *seem* brutal; but survival generally does."

"Of course," I said, nervously.

"But the splendid thing," he said, leaning forward in the stance of one indulging a great secret, "was that whenever I eliminated one of these nuisances, I gained his abilities. It was much easier to please my ape comrades, for instance, with sun *and* rain in my control: when they tired of the one, I could give them the other. Each gain after that led to a furthering of power, a conflict with other deities, many hard-fought victories. Slowly, over many millions of years, I came to control every process, not simply on earth, but in all existence. Do you have any questions?"

In hindsight, there were a million things I could have asked, at least. But his own question, and the weird story had put—it felt like a meatball in my throat. He was patient, though, and waited for me to recover. This is what I finally asked:

"But—do you think—might there be a . . . a *being* even higher in the ranks than you?" Not a particularly *safe* thing to ask, in hindsight, but it was the first thing that came to me. Luckily, he didn't seem offended, but shrugged his shoulders doubtfully and said, "If there is, I've never met him."

Again, I wasn't sure what to say. I thought about asking for an autograph, but was prevented by a distinct *gong* originating from somewhere beyond the room. God took a few big gulps of tea, his hand, I thought, shaking a little—probably from too much caffeine. He was quiet for a while, and then—

"I've summoned you here—Bill, was it?"

"Yes."

"Bill—for a very specific reason. Two, actually." He took the last dregs from his teacup, swallowed with resignation, and proceeded, I thought, as if what he said required more effort than he wanted to let on, and perhaps—a small sacrifice of dignity. "I need you to be the new Messiah."

I understood, then, why he hadn't offered me any tea earlier. I'd've scalded myself at this point.

"You see, Bill," filling not only his own, but a second cup, which he placed in my hands, "I've inflicted disasters, instigated wars, crammed heads full of kinds of hypocritical nonsense, and yet . . . I can't seem to encourage religious sentiment the way I once could."

There was such a dejected twist in his voice that, if it wouldn't've been gross presumption, I'd've consoled him.

"I'm my own nemesis," he went on. "To keep the devotion, the approval of the human race, I've given it every advantage I could think of. And now, content with all they have, and forgetting where it came from, attributing my efforts to natural forces— or worse, to *themselves*—" a chewing anger, now, in his voice, "they're prepared to discard me altogether. Not knowing I'm no myth or abstraction but, like them, real flesh and blood—and mortal, too."

He closed his eyes, and continued, "My castle in the air is reduced to this—dim hallway. My strength to that of *weak tea*."

He was now absolutely despondent.

"But you're going to help me. Some time ago—a few thousand years, perhaps—I asked the same favor of a man. He was . . . a little younger than you, but taller; and good enough to grant it. I gave him power enough to performs certain . . . magic tricks, really, which were taken, as I'd hoped, for miracles. The whole thing worked splendidly, and I soon reached a point of power and influence that before I'd only dreamed of. As time went on— more out of boredom than need, I think—I repeated the process, securing the help of several others, endowing them with special abilities. But they squandered the gifts, flaunting them like ringmasters, wasting them on all kinds of nonsensical pursuits. In horror, I watched telekinesis wasted on spoon-bending, rhetoric on *drama*. These con men made a lot of money, I'm sure. It was all an enormous disappointment. After that, I swore off messianic plans altogether—until very recently."

He lifted the teapot, then noticed I hadn't yet taken a drop from the first pouring. I'd been too befuddled.

"Apologies," he said. "This must be a lot to swallow."

"I'm sure it's very good tea," I said, then realized he meant the whole situation. "Yes, it's all a lot to—absorb," I said, quickly. And it was. I mean, a *lot*.

"No doubt, no doubt." He took another very deep breath, and continued. "What it comes down to, Bill, is—will you do it?"

It was my turn to take a very large breath, and a gulp of tea. For a while, I looked up at the ceiling, as if the pros and cons were pigeons in the rafters. *It'll be loads of work*, I thought. *Probably not much in it either, financially—you know, just one of those* SPIRITU-ALLY REWARDING *transactions.* I dawdled, and drank, and thought, and pretended to think. If I'd had a cigar on me, I'd've smoked it. I could tell that he suffered, impatient; but there was so much to think about. Finally, I made up my mind.

"I'll do it," I said. I was, after all, getting bored of the office job.

A sigh of relief. "I'm glad. Good. Thank-you." He looked me steadily in the eye for a moment, then, "Bill?"

"Yes?"

"There's one more thing."

I raised one eyebrow.

"I'd like you to ghostwrite my autobiography."

I raised the other.

"It'll serve as a revised and improved Bible for the current generation—only this time, with no balderdash. I realize, now, that using the same text for such a very long time was a mistake; the Testaments come across as a little too *antiquated* and Middle-east-ern these days. A good yarn and a few miracles might have amused the masses a thousand years back, but nowadays people require something more, something with grit and honesty and razzle-dazzle. A *confessional*. A *tell-all*. A *How I Did It, and How YOU Can Worship My Achievement (in Ten Easy Steps)*. Of course, that's only a working title." He refilled both cups, and clasped his hands together. "What do you say?"

This time, I blurted out my agreement, and left the hesitation for dessert. I'd always prided myself in my writing (did I mention I was a journalist?), and this *had* to be, let's face it, the ultimate scoop. It would be a whopper of a task, of course, but there are some people you just can't say no to. There was always the periph-eral worry, too, that if I declined, he'd frizz me with a thunderbolt or something. We shook hands, and celebrated with a nip or two of something that he removed from his desk drawer: brandy. *Brandy!* Talk about English!

I'd like to say writing the book was a cakewalk, but the thing took outrageously long to finish. There were a million stories and anecdotes to go through, not all of them interesting; and though God is, on the whole, a pleasant man, he's . . . changeable, and prone to occasional fits. In the end, the book—we decided *God's Autobio* was a punchier title—clocked in at around three thousand pages, cut down from an original five. It was loaded with killer material though, and we both agreed it would outsell the original, *easily*. After he trained me a little to act the part of a Messiah, he sent me back to Earth—the sensation was like being splashed with very cold water—where I was pleased to find myself, not mangled in the street where I'd left off, but near-recovered in Saint Anne's hospital, the manuscript safe in a valise at my bedside.

I wish I could say the rest is history—I *will* be able to, someday—but the whole business of being the Messiah and publishing the *Autobio* has been harder than I imagined it would be, especially since God decided that giving me any special abilities would be too "gimmicky." People tend to think I'm out of my skull, you know? Most of my converts are, I admit, kooks and mental patients. But finding followers has been easier than finding a publisher. I've submitted the manuscript to over fifty houses, and had nothing but rejection slips so far. They don't say what's *wrong* with the thing, mind you, just polite BS like "This isn't right for us," or "We have to be *very* selective, sorry." There was even one that said, "I'm afraid your manuscript simply doesn't complement *our* editorial preferences. *We* prefer works that are well-written, engaging, and intelligent. But this is only *our* policy. *Other* publishers may differ. *Best* of luck." Pompous ass.

I'll get there someday. Until then, I roam the cities, picking up followers where I can. There are several thousand of us so far. We call ourselves "Your Humble Servants." I thought it had an awfully *English* ring to it.

THE MAN WITH THE
RIDICULOUSLY HUGE COUPON

So this man walks into the store, the convenience store, steps up to the till, whips it out, right onto the countertop. And Janet and I just *look* at each other, eyes bugging out. Cuz neither of us has ever, I mean *ever* seen a coupon this big. *Huge*. And we see a *lotta* coupons between us, believe me. In New York City? *C'mon*.

So you're thinking big deal, right, what can a guy get with a coupon anymore, a buck off air fresheners? Well, yeah, basically—with your average, kiddy-sized coupon. But this was *one motherfucking enormous coupon*. Just colossal. And it's not like you can refuse a coupon, not if it's legit. So we just stand there, Janet and me, waiting for him to pick out his shit—Twizzlers, mozzarella, deodorant—and watching it pile up on the countertop, next to the huge coupon. It pretty soon gets so tall, the pile, that Janet here gets up on a chair and holds the top of it, me I hug the bottom, just to keep it from collapsing.

Do you remember that, like, mountain of garbage that caught on fire? The headline was something like, "Garbage Mountain Bursts into Flames: Thousands Killed." I remember falling on my ass laughing when I read that. I mean it was unreal, even though all those homeless kids, like, burned to death in garbage. The pile kinda reminded me of that for some reason—maybe because there was so much junk food in it—and I got to laughing again, which got *Janet* laughing, and I remember wishing the guy would hurry up before the whole thing toppled and buried us alive.

So we're waiting and waiting and finally he throws a vanilla air freshener on top of the pile, with a flourish, and says, "Done." And we ring it all through, all this shit, and the total's just *ridiculous*. Something like $17,000. But after we process the coupon, this mammoth coupon—keep in mind how big it was—*we* end up, like, owing *him* sixteen cents.

Anyhow, he's leaning on the counter, putting the sixteen cents in his pants, stalling a bit, trying to get a conversation going. So we just go along with it; I mean, he wasn't bad looking. Pretty soon he starts asking us about *our* coupons, and all the different stores we've been to and shit. I mean, it was presumptuous and everything, and I kinda wanted to tell him it was none of his fucking business. But he had, like, the bangs that go down over your eyes. Like that singer, remember? And a moustache.

Long story short, we end up back at his place. I was planning on saving my coupon till after I married, I mean that's the time to start saving, right, when you're buying a house and have a mortgage and shit? But the guy was pretty persuasive. Did I mention the moustache? And so I figure—it's only a coupon, after all—what the hell, why not? Those things expire anyways.

CHIMPANIONS

Sara got a Chimpanion. Helen got a Chimpanion. But when *Elsa Gartner* got one I said to myself, "Well that takes it!" Couldn't hold out another minute. Jumped into the car, never mind my hair, or the bed not being made, and drove straight to Wally's Department Store. $1,999.99, I could hardly believe it, a bargain sale price for a Chimpanion. I mean, I could barely afford it; but I could barely afford my house, my car, my credit card—you know, just add it to the pile. Raced home like a teenager, and lumbered in with the box (fifty, sixty pounds, if it was an ounce). "My God," I said to myself, setting it down, breathing hard. "My very own Chimpanion, at last."

Now, in case you haven't heard—if you've been in India or living with Zulus, or something—I'll explain about the whole Chimpanion thing. It wasn't a fad, really (fads are dumb), it was just—a really great invention. The sort of thing everyone could use, that everyone *needed*. When I think of what my life was like BC (Before Chimpanions), I cry, practically—I mean, it was so tough. So *ordinary*. It was no life at all.

Anyhow, Chimpanions (chimps + companions) were electric robot friends—pets, you might call them, though they were so much more than pets. They could follow instructions, almost anything you could think of, like "wash the dishes" (you had to say it in a loud, even tone), even hard stuff like "get the groceries" or "do my taxes." It was like having your own private butler. By the end, my Chimpanion (it took a while to train him—they start out wild) could dress me, brush my hair, even paint my toenails, which saved heaps of time. It was pretty sweet.

But "all good things . . ." as they say. We're AC (After Chimpanions) now, and life is murder. It all happened so quickly;

I hope I remember all the details, the important stuff anyway. Here goes.

I think the first thing my Chimpanion did, after I installed the batteries (they went in the rear end—funny, if a little indecent) and flicked the ON switch, was have a real rip-snorting tantrum. I was prepared for this—there was a warning on the box—but still, my heart was beating. I mean, the screams were so absolutely *real*. He even pulled out a few chunks of fur. Worst of all was when he jumped behind the sofa, and commenced chewing on the curtains—and they were *nice* curtains, floral, definitely not cheap. I was shouting things the whole time, of course, like "I command you to stop!" and "Bad monkey!" which any experienced Chimpaniowner (Chimpanion + owner) would've snickered at. If I hadn't been too excited to read the instructions in full beforehand, like you're supposed to, I'd've known you have to start every command with "Chimpanion," so he knows you're talking to *him*. So if I'd've said "Chimpanion, I command you to stop," he'd've done it. By the time I'd figured that out, he'd completely trashed the living room, smashed all the lamps, and swallowed five or six bananas, whole, from the fruit bowl. I was curious what would become of *those*, I can tell you; but I didn't find out until much later.

Eventually, I got him under control, and listening to commands. With both of us working, it didn't take too long to clean up the mess. I was pretty achy after that—pushing 70, after all—so I watched a little television (he seemed to like the same shows I did), then hit the sack. Chimpanions *do* sleep—that is, if you want them to. All you have to say is "Chimpanion, sleep," or "Chimpanion, good night." Stuff like that. But if you say "Chimpanion, lights out," they generally run around turning all the switches in the house off—you know, not *getting* it.

I hadn't really thought—it was so spur of the moment—when I bought my Chimpanion, where it would sleep. Luckily, there was an extra bedroom—small, and meant for a child (I'd never married). Trouble was, I'd filled it with dolls—my one great hobby, collecting them—life-sized porcelain dolls. You'd *swear* they were real. Expensive hobby, I'll admit; but without a family, a woman has to have something to waste her money on. *Beautiful* dolls. Anyhow, I must've had, at that time, well over a hundred—on the shelves, dressers, here and there on the floor, and all over the bed. So I took the Chimpanion to the dolls' room, and told him he was to share it, and be *very* careful with the dolls. Didn't react well to the idea, I'm afraid. At first, I thought there was another tantrum in store—but he settled down pretty quickly. It was the sight of so many eyes, I think, that made him jumpy. I've had strangers, honest to God, mistake the dolls for live children, so it was no wonder an Electric Chimp Companion would. I kissed him on the cheek (it was warm, from the electricity), and turned out the light.

It was a rude awakening, the next morning, to say the least. Started as a tinkling chime sound, which I didn't mind so much. After the explosion, though, I threw my robe on and bolted downstairs.

"OMG," I cried, saying it out the full way.

It was carnage—doll heads everywhere, smashed into bits, dresses ripped up. And over in the corner, curled up in a basket, was the Chimpanion, fast asleep—I mean, in Inactive Mode. I'll tell you, I thought about cramming him back into the box and getting a full refund. It's funny I didn't, considering how dear the collection was to me, and all the years it took to complete. But I'd already come to think of my Chimpanion as family, and you can't just take family back to the store. You sure can punish them, though.

"Chimpanion, wake up!" I said.

He did.

"Chimpanion—what have you done?" He didn't seem to follow—and I didn't expect him to, honestly. Because it wasn't an Approved Command. So he just gave a big wide grin, exactly like a kid. And I forgave him instantly. Of course, I made him clean up all the bodies; didn't lift a finger to help him, either; and put the whole thing behind me. I realized, then, that making a civilized creature out of my Chimpanion ("the goal of every responsible owner," as the booklet said) was going to be a challenge. But I was up to it.

2. TEA WITH MS. HUTCHINCE

A few days passed, and Chimpy—that was the name I settled on, and programmed him to respond to—made steady progress. By the third day, I'd trained him to fold laundry, and eat spaghetti with a fork (still wasn't sure what became of the stuff). But I was nowhere near ready to introduce him to company just yet. It didn't look like I'd have an option, though, because, one morning, without invitation—*Ms. Hutchince came to tea.*

Never much cared for Ms. Hutchince—so solemn and hoity-toity. Dressed like she was rich, but in reality she lived on a very fixed income. Her father was the town doctor, ages ago, an old grunion. "He'd pinch a penny till it bled," people used to say, and when he died, left his fortune to his only child—*on the condition*, the will said, *that she marry within twelve months of my expiration.* Otherwise the money went to Imperial Toffee. The old man was unusually fond of toffee. So she grabbed some local boy by the arm, hastily married him, hastily divorced (the will didn't say anything about *that*), and spent the rest of her days a spinster living off an inheritance. Never had to work a day in her life, though it's not like she could be extravagant. She came from a long-lived family, and had to make it last.

So anyhow, the next morning, there was a knock at the door. I opened it up, and there's that grave toad-face staring back at me. "I've come for tea," she says. "Oh. Come in—if you please," I answer. There's something about solemn people that makes everybody else solemn, too. And obedient. I'd've rather told her *scram*, but she was too respectable. It's like if the Queen showed up for dinner stinking drunk, you still couldn't say no. So I showed her into the living room, and went to the kitchen to make the tea. When I came back out, she was perched on the sofa, so I sat down in the armchair across from it (not the one beside it), laying the tray on the table between us.

"And how are *you*?" she asked, with a weak smile.

"Good, thank-you," I said.

"That's nice," she answered.

It got very quiet, so I said, "And you?"

"I'm well, thank-you."

A long silence, after that. *Really* awkward. I was wracking my brain for something to say next, when Ms. Hutchince raised an eyebrow (it was pencilled on) and said:

"And what do you call *this* creature?"

She was looking just over my shoulder, so I turned around and saw Chimpy wandering into the room, rubbing his eyes—cute, and something all Chimpanions are programmed to do after Short Deactivations (naps).

"Oh, it's my—Chimpanion," I said, not sure whether to send him away, or try my luck that he'd behave for once.

"Chim-pan-yun?" she said, pretending to've never heard of them. I just smiled to myself, knowing perfectly well that she'd been nosily making the rounds of every Chimpaniowner's house the last few weeks, trying to make it seem like she was just dropping in. Her stopping at my place proved it; I mean, normally she never gave me the time of day. The old bird probably couldn't afford a Chimpanion of her own, though of course she'd never say that. So I just played along.

"Chimp Companions," I said. "They're Electric Robot Friends—but awfully lifelike, don't you think?"

"Fairly," she said, taking a sip of tea, pretending to be barely interested.

I told Chimpy to have a seat, so he hopped up on the armchair next to Ms. Hutchince.

"Well, hello there," she said, in such a friendly tone, I was shocked—and amused. Chimpy just gave her one of his really big-sized, company grins. When she caught *me* smiling, she turned cold again, and said, stiffly:

"Does he *do* anything?" (As if she didn't know).

"He does *everything*," I said. "You name it, he does it."

"I see." She looked at the tea tray, and at her half-empty cup, and said, "Can he pour the tea. Without spilling it."

"Naturally," I said, even though he usually slopped a little. "Chimpy, pour her some tea."

He hopped off the chair, and filled her cup, luckily not spilling a drop.

"Thank you—*Chimpy*," said Ms. Hutchince. I could tell she was impressed, though of course she tried hard not to let on.

"Chimpy's a *great* help around the home," I said, pretending to sip some tea; I didn't want to run out and risk Chimpy fudging the refill.

"I'll bet," she said—in a sarcastic way, I thought.

"Extremely useful things," I said, starting to get irritated, "if you can afford one."

"But no substitute for a *husband*," she said, into her teacup

You old bitch, I thought. But all I said was, "Not everyone's the marrying type," practically grinding my teeth. And I couldn't resist adding, "How's *Mr.* Hutchince, by the way?"

She looked up like she'd heard a gunshot.

"I must be going," she said, rising. "Perhaps you and your *thing* would like to be alone."

"Chimpy, attack!"

I could hardly believe I'd said it, but I'd said it. And before I could stop him . . .

"Aaaah!" This was Ms. Hutchince, shrieking as Chimpy jumped her, knocking the teacup out of her hand.

It got pretty ugly after that. I mean, he *tore* her up—clawing, stomping, dragging her around the room, and taking every opportunity to put his sharp white teeth to good use. The whole thing lasted barely ten seconds, but there was lots of screaming (I mean *lots*), and then—well, quiet. Too much quiet.

"Chimpy, stop!" I cried. He did. As he turned around, I could see blood in his fur, staining his teeth (he was still smiling). "Chimpy," I said, shaking a little—"Chimpy, go upstairs. Go lie down." He made a pouty face, but obeyed.

From where I was standing, I could only see Ms. Hutchince's legs and torn slip sticking out from behind the sofa. "Oh boy," I said to myself. Of course I had to check things out, but couldn't bear to take more than baby steps, with the suspense, and knowing how bad the sight would be. At one point, I was barely moving at all, so I said to myself, "This is ridiculous," took a couple of big steps . . .

And there she was. Without being too gruesome, I'll just say there was *tons* of blood, and too many scratches and bite marks to count. It was a strange thing, too, to see such a prim, upright lady lying there with her clothes torn off, like she'd been ravaged. Ironical is the word. Even stranger, where her face ought to've been there was only a mat of dark hair—the back of her head. Her neck had been twisted all the way around and broken. I didn't need a doctor to tell me the woman was stone dead. But I thought, just to be *absolutely* sure she wasn't still alive, I should double-check. So I inched my way around the body, trying not to track around any blood. The way her head was angled, with the neck quite stretched out, and the chin bearing its weight, she seemed to be looking just over my shoulder, at the stairwell, like she'd done earlier. I superstitiously looked up—and there was Chimpy grinning back at me, like a kid.

"Go lie down," I repeated, a little louder. He listened this time. Chimpanions are programmed to respond to voice loudness, and generally take a shouted command more seriously than a soft one. I watched him vanish down the hall.

"Okay," I said, looking down at the body. Didn't have a clue what to do—I mean, I was *stumped*. It's not like I could call the cops. Police have never understood the complicated nature of Chimpanion ownership. It's not like I was innocent, either. I'd given the command; it was a slip of the tongue. But it's not like I told him to do all *that*. I mean, *attack* is different that *kill*, right? And I couldn't let them take away my Chimpy, either.

After a lot of thinking, it became pretty clear what I had to do. I knew Ms. Hutchince didn't drive, so as long as nobody'd seen her come inside, there'd be nothing to suggest she'd even come over. It's not like she was in the habit of paying me visits. It was taking a chance, but—I decided to get rid of the body. I knew time was of the essence (it generally is, in cases like this), so I called Chimpy back. With his help, I carried Ms. Hutchince to the bathroom, and hoisted her into the tub. Then I turned on the tap and—I was a little nervous about giving Chimpy a knife, especially such a big one; but what choice did I have? After the body was in fine enough pieces—Chimpy could cut through bone like butter—I scooped it into ice-cream pails, and put it down the garburator. Messy work, to say the least. Then the two of us spent the rest of the evening—I think we got to bed around two—cleaning up, looking for spots of blood, that kind of thing.

3. One Debutant

For almost a whole week, I didn't see the light of day, not once; too busy going through the Official Instruction Manual, and doing my best to civilize Chimpy a bit. Did you know Chimpanions were made from parts shipped in from Norway, Persia, and Swaziland? Only the best stuff. Anyway, by the end of the week—he could draw absolutely temperate bathwater, and was even learning to paint, a little—I thought it was high time Chimpy and the neighbours had a proper introduction. I mean, what's the use of having a Chimpanion if nobody *sees* him? It had to be in style, too.

Now, there was a whole line of clothing available—ChimpanionWare™—pants and tops, all kids of special outfits—"duds for you buds," as the catalogue put it. But I'd blown all my money on Chimpy himself, and couldn't afford any outfits (even if I wanted the Jade Kimono in the worst way). Lucky for me, I still had the doll clothes—not just the stuff that survived, but drawers full of extras. So I started going through them, changing him into stuff, even some of the girly things, just for fun. It was after lunch by the time we'd agreed on something—a beige business suit with a spotted tie—and even though I was starved, since I hadn't breakfasted, either, I couldn't wait to take Chimpy out and show him off to the neighbours.

So off we went. Lucky, by that point, that Mr. Law had revoked an earlier decree for owners to leash all Chimpanions out-of-doors. Cuz it would've been a shame, going through the suit trouble, not to mention combing his hair very carefully down the middle, like for a school photograph, to wreck it all with a dog collar, and a chain. I mean, *please*.

So off we went. I think Mr. McCrae was the first one we saw, watering his lawn. I waved. *Chimpy* waved. This shocked me at first; I hadn't given the instruction. Then I remembered something from the instructions, about the patented AdaptaChip™, how it lets the Chimpanions "observe, mimic, and *learn*." Which helps, you know, not having to shout orders all the time. Well we waved again, the both of us, but Mr. McCrae just stood there frozen, hose in hand, drowning a flowerpot. *Jealous*. So I smiled—you know, kill 'em with kindness—and Chimpy smiled too, with just the right sarcastic touch. *Remarkable*, I remember thinking.

Next a white van motored by—and in it Susan, the librarian, who waved back at least. At the sight of my Chimpanion, though, she turned her head away sharply, made it seem like she didn't give a damn (which was how I knew she *did*), and stepped on it. Which was so like Susan—you know, petty, small.

Click, click, click. It was John Parton—or Polo, as he called himself, as he *insisted* people call him—coming down his walkway in his leather boots, and poodley hairdo. To John—pardon me, to *Polo*—nothing was, *fine*, or *nice*, or *well and good*. It was always *charming*, or *gorge*, or some other frilly nonsense. Just once, I often thought, when you asked him how he was that day, couldn't he have said things were *damned miserable*, or *a little off*, or *shut up I have a headache*, like the rest of us? I mean, how on earth can you be *that* cheerful *all* the time? I suppose not having a wife to lock horns with or children to worry about helps, but still.

"Why, hello!" he cried, beaming, rushing up to me in his ludicrous booties. Then he leaned forward (I drew back, a little, but it was no use) and kissed me, twice—once on each cheek, like a Frenchman. Didn't enjoy that, I can tell you.

"*Charming* weather," he said next, grinning—"isn't it?"

"Oh, yes, it's—charming, all right," I said, forcing myself.

"*Delish*, even. Don't you think it's just *delish*?"

"It's delish, yes. Awfully."

I must've been grinding my teeth by this point, cuz Chimpy started doing the same, rubbing his RealistiPearls™ together till sparks flew off in all directions. *Adorable*. It calmed me a little, I think.

"What do you think of my new boots. Aren't they just *yummy*? Stole 'em, from a droll little shop in the West End."

"*Stole* them?" I said, horrified.

"Oh, yes," he said, smiling. "I'm quite the career criminal."

Something about his expression, here—and occasional giggle—that I didn't like. Made me feel—like I wasn't *getting* something.

"Stole this, too," he said, adjusting his belt.

"You don't say."

"Oh, yes. And the slacks. All stolen. It's the only way to go. The fashion, if you will."

"*I most certainly will not*," I said—worked up, I admit, but who could blame me? "I'm proud to tell you, Mr. Parton," he grimaced, "that all my clothes, humble though they may be, were *bought,* honestly, from *decent* people trying to earn a *decent* wage—" but here I stopped myself.

Calmly, like nothing, he brushed an invisible bit of lint from his shoulder, and said—

"It shows."

"Chimpy, attack!"

I hardly realized what I was saying. I mean, it just popped out. And before I could change my mind, Chimpy had leaped into the air, and landed right in Polo's arms, knocking the man—all 100 pounds of him—backwards, flat onto the ground, his head striking the walkway so hard that, if it weren't for the thrashing of his arms and legs afterwards, I'd've thought for sure it had smashed right open.

I looked around, in a panic. There was no one in the street, that I could see. No one gaping in windows, reaching for telephones. My first thoughts, of course, were for Polo, his safety—but I did a quick little 360, as a precaution. Even in that bit of time, Chimpy had moved from the man's chest to his head. He'd wrapped his legs tightly around Polo's neck and, holding his head still, on either side, by the hair, was . . . pretty much gnawing his face off. Like a corncob.

"Chimpy!" I cried (though not too loudly).

"Chimpy!" I repeated, grabbing the collar of his suit jacket, and tugging on it.

There was a *gurgling* sound, a *scraping*. The arms and legs moved more violently than ever. There was a smell of electricity—of singed flesh.

I was, despite myself, about to scream, when—the thrashing stopped. Immediately, Chimpy relaxed his grip, and turning about grinned at me, like a boy who'd been discovered at mischief. For once, the cuteness—and it *was* cute—didn't work all that well. I was *angry*. And I was afraid.

Drawing a deep breath, I turned, at last, and looked at Polo—at his face.

It was—completely eaten, and raw. I'd say a third of it—the forehead, and the jaw—was just bone. No lips to speak of. A hole, where the nose should be. To die in that way was—well, it was terrible. But then I remembered that Chimpy's legs had been around the man's neck, like a boa constrictor, all the while. So he likely—I like to think—died painlessly, of asphyxiation.

"*What have you done?*" I said to Chimpy, in disbelief.

He only looked up at me, quizzically, bits of flesh dangling from his chin.

I'm a rational gal. Plop me in the middle of Crisis Central, with folks bounding left and right like zapped rabbits, and I'm generally the one thinking "What's the fuss?" But I have to admit, this almost unnerved me. I mean, it was *close*. But I took a deep breath, looked around me, looked at Polo, weighed my options and—well, I knew what to do.

"Chimpy," I said, getting his attention (he was watching a butterfly). "Come closer."

Crouching down, I pointed at the dead man.

"Chimpy—eat," I said, making a pretend eating gesture.

But he just stood there, looking puzzled—probably because people aren't part of the Standard Recommended Diet for Chimpanions.

"Eat, Chimpy!" I repeated, looking around me, nervous someone would notice.

Chimpy titled his head to one side, like a puppy.

"See," I said, licking the man's hand—"delicious."

Chimpy itched his nose, then furrowed his eyebrows, then finally followed suit, giving the man's fingers a single lick. Of course, I'd hoped for more. But it was a start.

"Yum-yum," I said, rubbing my belly, pretending to eat down the length of Polo's arm, and move on to his torso.

Chimpy grinned. Silly thing seemed to find my antics amusing. But time was ticking. Growing desperate, I bit down hard on Polo's thumb, hoping he'd copy—which he did, stopping short, though, of going any further.

I swallowed hard—after all, it had to be done—and bit Polo's thumb, the end of it, clean off—and pretended to chew.

That did it. It was like a permission slip or something. In an instant, Chimpy set to work, eating from thumb to shoulder on one side, like a long stalk of celery. The speed, the efficiency, were just—wow. Then he switched to the left arm—and then the legs, the torso, and last of all (and I wasn't sorry to see it go, either), the head. Of course I spat the thumb out at the first opportunity.

I stood there a while, stupefied. I mean, that he could fit that much in him without swelling up. There was a churning noise, a whirring; finally, a bright "ding"—and a cube, of about twice the size of the sugar variety, dropped between Chimpy's feet. This was, I knew by then, the Pottycake™—an ultra-dense compress of waste material. Chimpanions *can* be fed, and double as waste disposals, too, but are so efficient as to produce only one Pottycake a month, on average, according to the manual—and this was his first. Reluctant but curious, I picked the thing up. Besides being mega heavy for its size, it was hot to the touch.

Oh—and it smelled like burnt carrots. Most Pottycake, regardless of what it's made of, is fully edible; though I don't regret not sampling it on *that* occasion. The question was—what to do with it? A non-option, taking it with me (way too heavy). I looked around for a place to hide it. Then it struck me that, maybe, I could feed the cube back to Chimpy, and see what happened. So I did (he took it hungrily), and after the expected whirring and dinging, out popped a cube of maybe a fifth of the size—but very nearly, I found, the same weight. I repeated this a few times, till I ended up with a cube no larger than a coarse salt crystal; and struggling into Polo's backyard with it, heaved it into his rain barrel with an impossible splash, watching it sink out of sight.

I had to be fast, now, I knew it. Pocketed the bit of thumb, then looked around me, the yard, to be sure there was nothing left behind, nothing to incriminate Chimpy. Then we dashed through the backyard, past the garden—and a really fine garden he had, too—and into the back alley. I was just about to sigh relief when—

"Hey, look!"

"A robot!"

"Awesome!"

More than a few people in this world describe themselves as "kid people," just as there are plenty of "dog people," "cat people," "ferret people," even. I'd mark my X, personally, in "none of the above." Can't say *why* exactly. Just something about kids—the atmosphere of chaos maybe—that makes a person . . . uncomfortable. *Really*. For a moment, I thought about high-tailing it in the opposite direction. But in no time, they'd circled us, and it was too late.

"Can he talk?" said one boy, stepping closer.

"Is it real fur?" said another, closer still.

"Can I have him?" said a third, reaching out.

I gasped.

"Is he nice?"

"Does he bite?"

"Whatcha feed him?"

I began to panic.

"What's *this* button do?" asked one boy, reaching for the Manual Shut-Down.

Chimpy looked up at me, nervously, and—I nodded my head. I didn't say a word, mind you; but I nodded my head. I won't deny it.

There's no point, I don't think, mentioning what happened next. I mean, describing it. It got pretty grisly. Noisy, too. I very nearly thought one of the boys (the one who'd reached for the button) would escape—he was halfway over the fence, already— when Chimpy snatched him by the ankles and—well.

There was no time, now, for anything but a quick escape. Already I'd heard a door slam, some mother call out, "Benny? Ben? Benjamin, darling? Ben-Ben? Benny?" So I grabbed my pet, all 88.6 pounds of him (the actual weight, as I'd learned), around the waist, and hauled him off, like a sack of potatoes, as fast as I could manage. Back through Polo's yard, around the corner, and across the street. As I slammed the front door shut, I saw Mr. McCrae, frozen, rake in hand, gaping back at me.

4. How it Ended

So there I was, back to the door, and my heart beating hard against it like a knocker. Chimpy stood facing me, hands at his sides in the classic Awaiting Further Instructions pose, which Chimpanions automatically assume indoors, in case they need to help with groceries, etc. I remember how innocent he looked, and how badly I wished, at that moment, to be an Electric Robot Companion, as well—the carefreeness, I mean.

You can't imagine, the halo of thoughts spinning round my head, how heavy it was, and how fast. It's not that I didn't know what to do, but what to do *first*. Change Chimpy out of his bloody suit and into clean clothes (the sailor suit, perhaps?). Hide him in the attic? Hammer out an *absolutely perfect* alibi? For a long time, I just stood there, thinking. But I was so exhausted from everything, so tired of running, and sick. I found myself sliding down the door, melting, till my bottom touched the carpet. I called Chimpy to me and, putting me arms around him, held him very tight, leaning on his shoulder, growing very sleepy, now, closing my eyes . . .

I awoke—and Chimpy auto-activated—to a sound of knocking. Won't have to tell you how alarmed I was. But then I thought, as the knocking had come from just above my head (I'd fallen asleep sitting up), it must be a child, only—the paper boy, if I was lucky, come for his monthly dues. Cautious—with the chain on—I opened the door, and peered out. But instead of a child staring back at me, I found myself nose to nose with a fairly stumpy policeman. Plus one of regular height, directly behind him. Of course I panicked, thought of slamming the door, leaping out the window, starting afresh in Swaziland, or something. But then I thought—I *knew*—the noble, womanly thing to do was to grin, as they say, and take it on the chin. To face the music. So that's what I did. There was really no way of escaping, besides.

I drew a deep breath, slid back the chain, and opened the door wide.

"Please!" I cried, throwing myself down at the officers' feet. "Have mercy on an old spinster!"

"Ma'am," began the first (short) officer.

"It's not *my* fault," I interrupted, "that they're so enticing, and that everybody wants one, and once you see somebody *with* one, you've absolutely *got* to have one, too."

"Ma'am," said the taller officer.

"And it's not *my* fault," I went on, "that there's over 365 different outfits available, most of them adorable, one for each day of the year."

"Ma'am," said one of the officers (I don't recall which).

"And it isn't *my* fault that—"

"You're not in trouble ma'am," said the first officer, laying a hand on my shoulder.

"What?" I gasped.

"We know what happened, ma'am."

"What happened," I repeated.

"With the children."

"The children."

"Are you all right, ma'am?"

"All right?" I said. "Yes. I think—I think I'll be just fine."

So this is how it all turned out. Just he day before, in Milwaukee, the officers explained, a Chimpanion by the name of Muddles had stormed into a law office—and shot ten attorney's on the spot. Just like that, without having been instructed (even by Remote-Voice Activation). This was a Texas Shoot-'Em Chimpanion, which always includes, besides an absolutely *adorable* hat, a revolver. The revolver's supposed to be *realistic*, though, not *real*, which it turned out to be. A "manufacturer's error" they called it, in the end. But understandable, I suppose, as the same company that made Chimpanions also made—and still does make—munitions. You know, bombs and stuff. And when a few more reports of killings came in, even as far away as Tasmania, governments the world over were ordering Chimpanions pulled off the shelves, retrieved from owners, and dismantled—poor things. No charges were being made against their owners, which was fortunate. I mean, you couldn't blame *us*, could you, for their electro-moral defect?

The hardest thing in my life, I think, was watching the policemen lead Chimpy, handcuffed, into the back seat of their patrol car and slamming the door shut. Even harder, as they drove away, watching him, with his head tilted to one side, Awaiting Further Instructions. But there were no more instructions to give.

Now, when I sit on the back terrace, or look out the front window at all the neighbours looking back at *me*, I can't help but think how *dull* life is—how *pointless*—without Chimpanions. They were a menace, I suppose. But I miss Chimpy, just the same.

I Am a Whale

I am a whale. I am an *old* whale. It's difficult to estimate, age, when you've lived so long. But I feel—I'm certain—that I must no longer be young.

We all seek something. What I seek is the Aegean Sea. This is the place where whales go, when they've grown old. Where others, grown old, have gone before me.

Aegean Sea. The very name is peace. Conclusion. I am told not everyone finds it, this place they seek. Many must die, or become lost, abandoning their search. But it's the dream, the last ambition of every whale, to find it.

There is really nothing like the ocean. Swimming as a whale swims. Near the surface, sun slanting in, illuminating. Or deep, and green, secret things stirring water, all around, moving and invisible.

The Aegean Sea is the best of all waters. Warm. Serene. Full of living and green things. Once you feel it, the water on your skin, this special lake of ocean, you're happy, it's said. Serene. In an instant.

The location of the sea is unknown. A mystery. We know the ocean, but the ocean is . . . incredible. There is, perhaps, an instinct in us, to find it.

Perhaps not.

There are suggestions, reports, of its place. But I am not sure whether to believe them. Wuurun, an old whale, told us. . . . *the door, between stone and stone, a lattice of waters.* Then he left us, singing.

He never returned.

But we seek, I seek, to find it. I'll know it, finally, when it's found. When I feel that special water, on my skin. And I grow serene.

I will find it, singing:

Luquist is the sea
algaen

green
        and peregrine

luquist
and swimmerless

osheen
        and peregrine

BLAKE'S BUTLER

So I became Blake's butler in—piss on the year. But I became his butler.

This is how it happened.

I was walking down 10th street. I think it was . . . dusk. Heading west. Sun in my eyes. Dammit, didn't have sunglasses. Broke 'em. Couldn't afford new ones. The economy, yada. Couldn't tell where the hell I was going, it was so bright. Didn't much care, either. Staggering.

Did I mention I had no sunglasses?

Then someone ran smack into me. Motherfucker. Hit the concrete, both of us.

Who the fuck do you think are you? I said.

Blake, he answers.

Blake who?

Blake the poet.

Blake the motherfucking poet, I thought. Whoop-de-doo.

Got up. Brushed myself off. But he just laid there.

Are you crying? Jesus!

I think you broke my rib.

Now how the fuck is that possible?

I'm fragile.

I thought: a poet. A fragile motherfucking poet.

Can you help me to rise up? he asks.

I did. Though it was a stupid way of putting it. Like, redundant or something. Bloody redundant.

So we stood there, in the middle of the sidewalk, people giving us the ugly mug as they passed by. Like it was any of their goddamned business.

Well, I didn't know what to say. Never busted a poet's rib before. I mean, I was sorry and all. But if you're that fragile you should stay the hell indoors and not bother anybody.

About to walk off when he turns and says:

Will you be my butler, brother?

Holy fuck, I thought. I was not expecting that. I was seriously not expecting that. Less surprised, I think, if he'd pulled a rabbit out of his ass. I mean, shit.

Long story short, I said yes. My job sucked ass. And he was
offering ten bucks an hour—a helluva lot better than the 8.50 I
was getting scooping up shit at the pet shelter. The guy was ecstat-
ic, asked me if I could start "instantly" and I said what the hell, ok,
nothing better to do.

So we were walking to his place. I don't mind a good walk.
Never had a car, so you get used to it. But after forty minutes I
was thinking, jeeze man, couldn't we've just taken the bus? And if
you've got the dough for a friggin' butler, a taxi can't put you out
much, right? But unless you're, like, a senator or something, you
can't just take a job and start bitching straightaway. Feet were
killing me, though. So I said something round-the-bush, like:

Quite a long ways, ain't it?

Hmm? What? Yes. Very . . . far, is all he says.

Brought up the nice weather, not like I gave a flying fuck, just
being conversational. But all he does is tilt his head up, staring at
a seagull, I think, not saying nothing, just walking with his chin
sticking straight out. Guess he was having one of those "poetic
reveries" you hear about. Had to stop him from plowing into a
trash can. Half-suspected at the time, I gotta admit, he was stoned
or something.

So we were hoofing it. And the further east we went, like, the
divier things got. Bit off the topic, but ever notice that rich people wear too much shit? Like, layers and layers of shit. Jewelry and
accessories, yada. Suit and tie on a hot July day. Well, besides the
buildings and the trash and shit, I could tell things were going
downhill from just that. Dudes went from the upright, dressed-up,
clean-shaven type to shirtless, hunched over, scruffy. Like that
evolution of man diagram in reverse. With the monkeys, you
know? And I'm thinking, what kinda fucking detour is this? I was
gonna say something, but I thought, you know, maybe the guy

really is on something—poets, you know—and needs a bitta "inspiration." Cuz it was the right neighbourhood for that, I tell you. I mean, I'm from the Iron Triangle, which is kinda like the armpit of the city; but this—man, this was the groin. So I was a little surprised when he stops in fronta this crumbling brownstone, and pulls out a house key.

Welcome, he says, opening the door, to my humble abode.

Humble's right. The place sucked ass. Dumpy one bedroom. Dusty as hell. I think there was one light bulb in the place. A card table, only. Pair of armchairs, the stiff-backed Ebeneezer type, you know what I mean? A fireplace, at least. And a piano, the old upright kind. Not in tune, either, as I'd find out. Nothing worse than an outta tune piano. Drives me fucking nuts.

I remember looking around and thinking, this guy can afford a butler? And he must've sensed it cuz he darts over to this urn-looking thing on the mantel and reaches inside and pulls out, like, $500 cash.

A week's wages, he says, passing it my way. Good enough for me. Money talks, right? Genius of the guy, really, keeping his money there. An urn. Can't trust a bank these days. And as far as thieves go, you'd have to be a pretty sick freak to stick your hand into something that might have, like, geezer dust and teeth and shit in it. Bloody smart. Could've done without the puns though. Cuz the guy got into the habit of saying shit like, "you certainly *urn* your keep," when he'd pay me and shit. Bloody annoying.

Anyway, I won't go into all the pissy training details, but you can bet that turning a Brooklyn roughneck into a half-assed butler was a pretty long row. Didn't think I'd make it, sometimes. The swearing was a problem, for him. Touchy. Must've had, like, Catholic parents or something. But I got better, anyway. There were words I was allowed to use. Like "sugar" for "shit." Felt like a complete tool, though, dropping a glass, and saying, "Aw, *sugar*." Would've died, man, if my buddies had heard me. Never live it down.

It wasn't long before we'd settled into an easy routine, Blake and me. I can't tell you everything, cuz it would bore your ass off, and I'd be here all day. A few things, though.

He wasn't one of those early risers. None of that watching the sun come up in rapture bullshit. Usually shuffled outta bed 'round 10:30 or 11:00. Wore a dress shirt, even to bed, but meant for a pretty big guy, down to his knees almost. Always had pear halves or clingstone peaches for breakfast, from a can—never any fresh stuff 'round the place—couldn't afford it, don't imagine. Ate lotsa oatmeal, but like for dinner and shit, which was weird. Never touched booze, so, you know, it wasn't *that*.

His hair. Holy fuck. I must've spent . . . *half* my life doin' the guy's fuckin' hair. There was a whole routine to that, too:

He'd come outta the bathroom—the guy spent most of his waking hours in the tub—then sit down, in a towel, at the piano. He'd start twiddling away at the keys, not really playing any kinda tune, so far as I could tell, but just twiddling. Which was my cue to grab the pomade, this big orange tin o' gunk, and the "fine fine comb," as he called it, and get behind him.

Man, did I hate that pomade. Greasy shit. The smell was just god-awful. Like gasoline. Now, I don't mind a gas smell if it's just at the pumps or something, kinda like it in fact, but getting it all over your hands is another thing.

So I'd comb his hair back with the fine fine comb, then take a wad of pomade, rub it between my hands to get it going a bit, it was stiff as wax, and then try to rub the stuff into his hair without ripping it out, which was bloody tough. Like buttering bread with cold butter, like right outta the fridge. When people give me cold butter, I feel like ripping their goddamn throats out. Muffins are just as bad. There is nothing worse than cold butter on a warm, crumbly muffin.

Anyway, if I was getting too rough, he'd let me know by sliding up the keys a bit, and playing all high notes. Then I'd be gentler, and he'd ease back down to his standard twiddle twiddle. Something about the guy. Just couldn't be direct. Like saying what you think would be too easy. Not poetical enough. Or maybe he just thought he was being polite or something. But I'm a pretty tell it like it is kinda guy, and when your answer to something like, "Coffee too dark, chief?" is to twirl your finger in your hair and glance up at the moon, well, it's fucking aggravating.

Anyway, I'd get all the gunk in his hair, then I'd cover it with a hot towel for 5 or 10 minutes. Then off comes the towel, and—Jesus. I mean, he looked fucking ridiculous. Like Count Dracula or something, all flat and slicked back. You'd think he'd wanna grow it out, or let it all dangle, you know. It wasn't very poetical at all. But the guy *insisted* 'on it.

Okay, there's this conversation we had once, just wanna get it in before I forget. We were sitting at the card table. I was playing solitaire, and Blake (he never touched cards, either) was just sitting there, staring up at the ceiling like there's spiderwebs or something, and then—

Where is fancy bread? he asks me.

In the cupboard, I tell him.

Where is fancy BREAD? he repeats.

In the CUPBOARD, I say, getting a bit irate.

WHERE is fancy BREAD? he asks again, looking a little hot himself.

IN THE MOTHERFUCKING CUPBOARD, FUCK. And I threw the cards right in his face, stormed off. We didn't talk for a week.

Oh shit—the *muffins*. His favorite food, bar none. If I spent half my life doin' Blake's hair, I must've spent the other half baking him muffins—and I'm no cook, believe me. Carrot muffins, blueberry muffins, and that choky bran kind that, like, give you the shits or whatever. Anyway, the first batch I made, the bran kind, a little burnt, a bit lopsided, whatever, but still eatable, I plunk one down on the card table. And he looks up, Blake, and says, Could you cut the crust off, please? So I take the wrapper off, thinking that's what he means, right? But he shakes his head, and says, The *crust*. Please. And I'm, like, what the fuck, so he grabs the butter knife, cuts a little round ball, like a donut hole, outta the center of the muffin, slaps some butter on top, and pops it in his mouth. Then he pushes the rest—like three-quarters of the fuckin' muffin—aside, and says, Dispose of this, please. I couldn't fuckin' believe it. I mean, the waste. So insteada just chucking it, I pick it up, choke it down. Like, just to spite him, I guess. *Crust.* Bullshit.

Anyway, that's how my days went—and if they sound tedious, believe me, they were. Almost as bad as the nights. Cuz from, like, 7:00 till midnight, all the guy did was *read*. In *silence*. Worse, he expected me to follow suit. Get me to push the table and chairs in fronta the fireplace, get it cracklin', grab an armful of old books off the shelf 'at random,' and plunk 'em down on the table between us. And he'd just grab one, open it up, and read it through. Trouble is, I'm not much of a reader. And total silence, like, gets on my nerves. Never got much of that growing up, in my neighbourhood, I tell you. But that first night, I remember thinking, like, better make the best of it, so I reached over and grabbed a book, opened it up—and the title was like, *Instruments of Moral Decay*, or something. Shit, I thought, this is gonna be a long night. And it was. But I learned a little trick after that. Art books, I found out, often have, like, paintings of naked fat chicks in 'em; so I always made sure to include a few of those 'at random,' every night. Not like I'm a cushion-pusher or anything.

Once the boss turned in, I was free to do whatever; but when you're waiting hand and foot on somebody all day, hey, by midnight, you're kinda bushed. There was a dive bar practically across the street, though it was the kinda place where you had to brush the syringes off your seat before you sat down. Sometimes, I'd go there for a round or two, maybe get lucky. Usually just hit the hay, though.

Oh in case you're wondering, in a crampy one-bedroom with no couch where I slept, it was on a floor mat in fronta the fireplace. My back's still feeling that, I tell you. Every other night, Blake would say, You're more than welcome to sleep with me, brother. But I'm, like, no fuckin' way. The floor it was.

Listen, I know he was a famous poet and everything, and that's why you're giving a bum like me the time of day. But I've gotta admit, I really didn't give a flying fuck about his poetry. Not many people did. The only 'admirers' I ever saw drop by were, like, Jehovahs, and this old dude who I'm pretty sure was schizophrenic. Maybe that's famous by poetry standards.

But this one time. We were sitting by the fire. He rips a blank page outta the book he's reading, takes a pencil out of his pocket (the guy *never* used a pen), and starts writing. Like a *demon*. Three minutes flat, I swear, and he's done. Can I read you my new poem, he says to me. And I'm like, yeah, okay, whatever. So he reads it. And it's like—I'm in some kinda trance. I mean, beautiful, beautiful poem. I am not ashamed to say it, but I got a little teary-eyed. And when he catches me, he just smiles, folds up the paper, and throws it in the fire. Doesn't say a word. I've never understood why he did that. Why he'd wanna do that. I guess that was the one time.

When Blake died, I was polishing the silverware. He said he was going out for a bit, and I should stay behind and polish the silverware. Remember thinking that was kinda odd, cuz he didn't HAVE silverware—just your ordinary stainless steel shit. Plus he'd never asked me to do that kinda thing before. Maybe I knew something was up, but—you just never knew what this guy was gonna say or do. Kinda all over the place, you know? Like he was bipolar?

So he goes out, I flip on the radio, kinda kick back for a while, the cat's away, right, and when I finally get around to the "silverware," it's maybe 3 hours later. And I'm just laying down a spoon when a voice comes on the radio and says, The body of renowned local poet William Blake has been recovered from the East River. Eye witnesses—who observed the poet crossing the Brooklyn Bridge—report that he stopped just short of the north tower, climbed onto the railing, and gazing upward 'in an abstract manner,' jumped into the river. Police are calling it a probable suicide.

Fuck, I remember thinking. Fuck. I said it out loud.

I mean, it was so unexpected. Didn't strike me as the type. A little flighty, yeah—but I mean, he was a fuckin' poet. Jesus. It shook me up. I guess—I cared more about the guy than I realized.

Man. And it was good money. Not great money, but decent money, you know? Jesus.

So after I got my shit together, I thought—I mean, I was just curious—I'd take a peek in the urn, just to see what was left. So I open it up, and . . .

Empty. Not a penny.

I remember thinking, hope he didn't axe himself over *that*. Cuz we've all been there. Hey, I'm a good guy, I'd've taken a pay cut if it meant keeping the guy alive. Course, *where* the money came from's another question. I mean, he printed a poem here and there, but that's not gonna pay the bills, let alone a fucking butler. Jesus.

He was kinda like—you know people who are 'independently wealthy' and don't really have to do shit just go to the opera and look good in earrings and shit? This guy was like, independently poor. An old lady on a fixed income, with a canary. That's what it was like.

He was probably on welfare.

The End of Everything

So basically, it was the end of everything. The world. I'm not gonna get into how it came about; it's a long story, and like most long stories, boring as hell. It was nothing fast, spectacular, silver screen, like a comet or a flood or something. But it did come—eventually. It came . . . and there we were.

When I say "we," I don't mean the human race. Cuz I was the only one left, I'm pretty sure. I mean me, the magpie, and the whale. *The whale, the magpie, and I.* Still trying to use proper grammar. Though I'm pretty sure Max—that's what I call the magpie—doesn't much care.

Maybe it was just a fluke that we survived. It could've just as easy been a leopard, an oyster, and a swan. Or nothing at all, no one. But I've got a theory.

I'm smart. A smart guy. No da Vinci, no. But still, pretty smart. Whales, are smart. Probably the smartest things on Earth. I've heard. And it got me thinking that, maybe, the smart survive. The meek inheriting the Earth and all. In the end.

But then I wondered about Max. How to explain him. I'd just assumed, right, that birds are dumb. Small heads. Sequin eyes. Twittering. I was sitting in the grass, one morning, watching Max building a nest. And he was so precise with it, so careful, always picking just the right size of stick, thickness of mud. And I was like, maybe I've underestimated the guy.

Seemed a bit of research was in order. For that, I had to go into the city. Don't like to waste gas, if I can help it. But sometimes, you know, curiosity. It gets the better of you.

Well, it took a while, but I finally tracked down the answer in one of the shuddering libraries, in a black leather book—at first I thought it was a Bible—called *The Family Corvidae*. Not much in the way of entertainment value, no, but it gave me my answer:

"The corvids—i.e. the ravens, crows, magpies, and several species of smaller passerines—are considered the most intelligent birds on Earth."

So there you go. Smart, all of us. The survivors. I smiled to myself, shut the book, and got the hell out of there, just in time. Cuz the whole place shuddered to the ground. Folded over. Close call.

So I took the book home with me. I live by the sea. My house is . . . right by the sea. It's good to have at least one book. Read a bit every day, in bed. Learn something every day. Like— did you know magpies can talk, be trained to talk? Better than parrots. Only they're so homely, no one bothers with 'em. Life, right?

I taught Max to say over a dozen things. Pretty bird. Happy birthday. Curse word or two. Not that it was easy. Took a lot of repetition, weeks, to get anything. But once he learned, Max, he never forgot. It was just like having a radio. But not a very good one.

Did you know . . . the magpie is one of the few species that can recognize itself in a mirror? I didn't. Till I read it. But I should've guessed it. Cuz Max would perch on the backs of chairs, or the bathroom faucet, just to get a glimpse in one, a mirror. Stared at 'em for hours. I hadn't realized, how vain he was.

The sound of the ocean, at night, it's amazing. Puts me to sleep every time. I'd never seen the ocean before.

Max and I, we spend our days combing the beaches, straggling. There's still some pretty neat wreckage. A flute, one day. Tambourine, the next. Then . . . a sousaphone. I wish I knew how to play.

The end of the world's not so bad, really.

The best thing is the whale rides.

POSSIBLE FICTIONS

TONIGHT

I thought, D, I mean I seriously thought this city would save my life. I don't know why. I just—it seemed possible, then. Before, when I'd drive around the city, see people—young people, my age, just walking together, going in and out of apartments together—I felt . . . like I was missing out on something.

It was a big change for me. A real change. Such a small place, barely a town. A village, probably. The big city.

There's freedom, being alone, a new town. But it's not like you'd think.

This is a lonely city.

In my building there's maybe ninety, a hundred people. Don't know one of 'em. See 'em on the stairs, sometimes—no elevator—and nod, maybe. They come home, close the door. It's what I do, too. Close the door, lock the door. I just wanna knock on a door, when I'm going by. Say hi or something. But it would be just . . . too weird, you know?

I've seen so much in this city, D. You wouldn't believe it.

This man, he goes by my window, back and forth, every day. With a bunch of cans. Sells 'em, buys a drink, sells some more. If he can find 'em. If he can't, if his luck's bad, he doesn't go past so often; and when he does, he's like, shaking, seriously shaking, all over. Crying, sometimes shouting, if he's bad. I think that's—they call it the DTs, right? You wanna empty your wallet into his hands. I've done it, a couple times; but you can't always.

There's hundreds and hundreds of people like that out there, D. Hundreds and hundreds.

Sometimes I just sit here all night.

It's strange, things you'll notice. In the morning, there's more men around, always. Afternoon, women, older people. At night, till pretty late, sometimes, look, it's kids. Too young to be out themselves, this late, this neighbourhood. But there they are. Sometimes there's someone . . . down the street a bit, straggling; and maybe that's a mother, or father, they never seem to look back.

Hansel and Gretel.

People run out of options. They try everything and do everything they think'll make them happy, make things work out. But sometimes nothing does. For some people.

Do you ever wonder, D, why life just doesn't work out for some people? I mean, take a group of people who grew up in the same place, had the same food, school, great parents, all that. And some of 'em'll go on and have families, nice houses, good jobs. But the rest. . . .

Like this kid from my class. Total ace. Like, a genius or something. Born for greatness. He was studying . . . physics, I think, last I saw him. Then I hear, not long ago, he's over on the east side, sleeping in the park, getting high all day.

How many guys out there have the same story?

You can sit a marble on the floor and think you'll know which way it'll run. You'll be wrong, though, a dozen times over.

So this guy shot himself through the neck last week, in my building. Police everywhere. Women screaming. When I was a kid, I used to wonder why people, how people could ever do things like that. Just couldn't understand it when I'd hear about it, see things on TV. I've learned a lot, D, since I've been here. You learn things you always wondered about, and you learn things you hoped to God you'd never find out in your life.

It's a rough city, a poor city. It's not all rough, though, not all poor. Not everywhere. But the only part I see, most people see. It's like . . . does it matter that you live in a mansion if you never leave the porch? Or if you're just a servant or something there, and nothing's yours?

There's this peach, so ripe, just perfect, and you can't touch it. You can't touch it cuz it's not for you. And you sit and watch somebody else come by, and pick it right in front of you. Maybe somebody who didn't even want it that bad. They take a bite, let it fall. And you just sit there, feeling sick.

What time is it?

Night's always the same time, anyways. Doesn't matter if it's 8, or 10, or 4 in the morning. It's dark, and it's quiet.

When the sun goes down, you start thinking. It's bright enough, and it's busy enough before, it's just . . . you move from distraction to distraction. Talking too much, doing too much. Sometimes I just sit here, watching, thinking, all night. Not always good stuff, D. I guess it makes you gloomy. It makes me pretty gloomy, sometimes. Philosophers must've been . . . unhappy people.

I don't know if I get so sad from what I see around me—cuz it's a sad world, D, really—or if I'm just a sad guy. Maybe seeing the bad side of things.

Everything could really be better than it seems.

That kid over there, going up the steps. Does living in that kind of place get him down? Or does he think it's like—it's a pretty big old building—a castle, or something, maybe. You don't know what kids are thinking. A prince in his castle.

I just—it gets hard to see the good in things, in people. It gets really tough, sometimes.

Maybe there's something wrong with me, D. It could all be in my head. And maybe I'll wake up one morning, blue sky, and everything'll be just fine. Cuz it always was.

I hope so, D.

★

The sun's coming up.

Cougar Granny

I'd made the trek many times, hoping always to meet him, waiting long hours to meet him, yet turning back in the end, each time, defeated. But that morning, when I heaved open my window, leaned out, and I breathed in . . . I *knew*. I knew, children, and I readied myself.

So on my hands and knees, I pushed open the door of my cottage.

The strength in my legs is gone. My sight, is all but gone. I see neither colour, nor shape. But . . . light, only, and dark. The distinction.

Running from my door, around the house and down the hill, into the trees, is a path. The stone is . . . limestone, and white. A very bright stone. I can *see* the stone by its brightness. This is how I move about the yard, tend my garden. Following brightness. An old moth.

I moved along the path, feeling my way. The stones were warm to the touch. It was a good hour. Mid-afternoon. A bit later, even. They'd been killed, the children, always, around the supper hour, or just before. But not again. I'd find him, the killer, at last. And it would be the end.

On my back, secured with rope, was a shotgun. Winchester, 1887. Twelve gauge. An old shotgun. A good shotgun. I'd slipped a shell into the breech, before strapping it on. This was one of only three shells, now, in my possession. The others I slipped in my pocket—doubting, though, I'd need them. One shot would be all, or nothing.

I made my way around the house, down the hill. It was . . . a still afternoon, in early fall. An advantage. Once the birds had quieted down (there were only a few—sparrows, mostly, and crows) it would be silent. Every movement, every step, however soft, I'd hear through the leaves. And I'd be ready.

The stone ended at the bottom of the hill, though the path itself continued. It carried on, a dirt trail, through the woods for a mile or so, and down into the village.

So I moved from warm stone to cool earth, pressing on twigs, on insects, my own handprints, the marks and grooves of my knees from past trips. It's a good place, this stretch, for berry picking, trapping rabbits, and partridges. I know it like my cottage. I travel it often. All the way to the village, sometimes, where they laugh, and scold me, give me tea, insist on pulling me home in a wagon, like a child. I'm an old woman, but strong. Only my legs are weak.

I breathed in—this is as good as seeing. I listened—this is better. I smelled sweet grass, and moss. I heard . . . the dry flutter of maple seeds falling. Many things. But not the enemy.

I moved on. Listening, crouching, tasting the air. A prairie snake.

It was a half hour, I think, before I stopped to rest. Everyone needs to rest. I sat down in the dirt. And as I sat, a *sound*. Like . . . a kettle boiling over. Or an old woman's wheezing. Like *this*. Do you know it? *The sound of a cougar, low to the ground, and hissing.*

I won't pretend that I was unafraid. I'm a brave woman. My mother a braver woman still. But when I trembled, it was half, only, out of fear, and half—*eagerness*. Almost . . . joy. The time had come, at last. I was face to face with the enemy.

The sound again, just ahead, of steaming water. I was as still as still water. You've been told many times, children, when confronted by a wild thing, not to look into its eyes. Yet it's more than that. You must not let the beast look into *yours*. My eyes are useless to me, nearly. But I made sure to close them. This was a beast twice my size. Many times my power. If I was to stop him, I would have to move. And yet—I would have to move slowly. Slowly, with amazing caution. And hope . . . each second was not the second he'd bound—either onto me, or off, into the woods—and the chance would be gone, perhaps forever.

With one hand, and slowly, I unfastened the knot of rope at my waist. With the other, as carefully, I reached behind me for the shotgun. I was about to grasp it, the stock . . .

There was a long, a low growl—at my side, now, my right. I had to decide whether to hold still, or move for the gun. When I breathed in, now, I smelled . . . a furred scent, animal scent. He was very close, the killer. Too close, I thought, for sudden movement.

So frozen, I waited. A minute, two minutes. The growl came again, from behind. He was circling me, the cat, like prey. I would not be his prey.

There was . . . pure silence. I could not tell where my enemy stood. A panic took hold of me, shortened my breath. I could hear, now, my heart, my rubber heart, bouncing, and—

A crushing of leaves to my left. I breathed, more freely. It was a good chance, while he was moving, perhaps looking away, to take hold of the gun. I pulled back the hammer, latched it, rested the butt against my shoulder. I rose onto my knees, pointed the shotgun in the region of the sounds. And I waited.

I could have taken a shot. There was time, and chance, to pull the trigger many times, while he moved through leaves. It's difficult enough, though, to strike something moving, for one with strong eyes. I needed to be sure of a hit. If I missed, the enemy would run off. He would kill again, and soon. I had one chance, only.

So I followed his movement, his scent, staring blindly down the rib of the gun. Ahead of me . . . the snapping of a twig. Then silence.

I squeezed the trigger.

The noise shook me, children, like cold water. But it wasn't the shot. Just . . . before I'd pulled it in, the trigger, a noise—stopped me. Startled me, I'm afraid. There aren't many things, at my age, that can. But the scream of a cougar, so close at hand, and unexpected, it shook me. The butt of the shotgun slipped from my shoulder, struck my knee painfully.

In an instant, though, I had the gun back in place. I recovered myself. I cursed myself for my weakness. It couldn't happen again.

I was first afraid, and then angry with myself. And determined. I wouldn't fail. The urge to shoot was very great. I had to be sure, though, of his position. I listened, but could hear only the wind which had risen, stirring the leaves. I could hear nothing but leaves. I grew impatient. What if the villain had wandered off? I turned my head, my ears, my nose, in all directions, but could sense nothing. I rose higher on my knees, like an animal when it stands, and—

I was struck. Across the face. My lip, here, my nose. These marks, these scars, children, tell tales. I was struck, and fell back in the dirt. The gun I nearly dropped. Very nearly. Any moment, I knew, the cat might be on top of me, his jaws at my throat.

And then, as before—a scream. The eerie scream of a cougar—two cries, short and fast, then a third, longer, and lower. A frightening sound, children. Yet I was unafraid. I was unafraid, even as the scream was repeated, more loudly, closer at hand. And more loudly still.

The time had come. It was *his* time—or it was mine.

I pointed the gun at the source of the sound—a few yards, it seemed, from where I lay. I pointed, and I pulled the trigger.

A good hunter, children, knows he's hit his mark, even before his eyes give him proof. The blast was so loud, and echoed so, that . . . there was no chance to hear any cry, any falling down or retreat. But I knew that, if I crept forward a few paces, I'd find him there, on the ground.

So my hands touched the animal, the great mass of fur, on its side. I rubbed him over, searching for the wound, stopping, at last, at his nose, where there was only—a hole. Warm blood rushed out, like a rivulet. The shot, a good shot, through his skull.

And yet he lived. Just so. Every odd second, a limb, or his head, would twitch. I thought—of reloading the gun, of finishing him. But I knew—his breathing had grown so rapid, and small— death would come, in a moment, only, or two.

So I leaned over him, stroking his fur, wonderfully soft. I spoke to him. I spoke . . . a prayer. Though what I did was neces- sary, children, though it needed to be done—still, I was sorry. I am always sorry. It's a shame, always, to take a life, even when it's nec- essary.

A second, two seconds, and his breathing stopped.

That's him, behind me, on the wall. Everything but the eyes is real. Those are of glass. He killed three of your friends, your cousins, in one summer. It could have been many more.

THE BLUE ROOM

Warden stood there, thirty feet below dust devils and the hot sun, in one hand the rope, in the other a lantern—turned low, for the moment, to save oil. He stood on a round wooden platform so small, to fit the narrow shaft, that there was barely room enough for his feet. There was a hole in the center of the platform, and running through it a rope knotted at the bottom and rising upward, out of the shaft, over a wooden crossbar, and around a spool which, turned via a crank one way or the other, raised a passenger, or lowered him.

The rope. Holding it tightly with one hand, Warden wished that it was only a *little* thicker—and not so frayed in places. He wasn't a heavy man, no; but there was the backpack full of tools and water adding to his weight, and the strain. At nearly thirty feet below the surface the rope was, after all, the only thing that kept him from plunging another fifty, to the bottom.

And men did fall. *Occasionally*, Warden was told. But something about the way Harthoorn, the old man, had said this—lowering his voice a little, dodging his eyes—caused Warden to suspect it might be oftener than that. But Harthoorn assured him it was a rarity, happened only out of carelessness, and moreover hadn't happened to anyone *he* had ever worked with. Warden had very nearly asked his friend what happened to the men who fell, but checked himself. Surely, considering the depth, most of them died in an instant; and as for the others—Warden preferred not to think of the others. He would keep quiet, do his job. It was too early, on a hot day, for asking many questions.

Holding the lantern out a little further, Warden scanned the walls of the tunnel, hoping, however unlikely at this depth, to light on a telltale flash of blue. He could see a few quartzes—a good size, admittedly, but hardly worth taking. One or two spots showed signs of being scratched at by other hopefuls; but considering the danger—he'd have to let go of the rope, and balance perfectly on the unsteady piece of wood—he thought it best not to bother. He'd been still for nearly a minute—Harthoorn had forewarned him of a midway break, essential to his age—but now, his rest over, the squeal of the hand crank resumed, and the platform again began to lower.

It seemed faster, now, the descent. Warden wondered if this was because Harthoorn worked harder after his rest, or whether, with the tunnel darkening as it deepened, it became more difficult for him to gauge his speed correctly. With each several feet of decline came another change—of temperature, moisture, of light. Soon he could see nothing but the lantern itself, and beyond that the odd crystal glimmer that was so much like the twinkling of stars that he felt, for a moment, that he must be in an open field, with the whole night sky spread before him.

It seemed he'd never reach the bottom. The hole was close to eighty feet deep, and it would take, Harthoorn had told him, more than twice as many turns of the handle to deliver him safely to his destination.

"But I'll give you a holler when you're close," the old man had explained. "I've a . . . feel for it." In fact, it was only a moment after hearing his friend's shout of *very soon* that he did strike bottom, with a greater jolt than he'd expected, and an eruption of dust which, if it couldn't be seen, could certainly be felt.

When he'd finished coughing, rubbing dust from his eyes, he swung the bag of tools from his back and propped it against one side of the shaft. He turned the lantern up a little, as it had suddenly become even darker—but this was because Harthoorn, leaning over the mouth of the shaft, had blotted out the sun completely.

"All's well, friend?" he called, squinting into darkness.

"Yes."

"Very good. And you need nothing?"

"No. No, I don't think so."

"Then I'm off. Some little business, in the village. Eleven, I think, I'll come wind you up. We'll go for a drink, ah? And you'll show me your treasures."

"I'll do my best."

"Good, good," Harthoorn replied, in a smiling way, not that anything of his face could be seen clearly. Then his shadow withdrew—the shaft brightened slightly—and his eyes adapting, Warden took stock of his surroundings.

Though the shaft itself was a narrow one, at a distance of six feet from the bottom where the walls had been picked at by many men before him, it broadened a little, so that it had, on the whole, the shape of a long-necked chemical flask. There was a cavity on one side of the flask, which proved, when Warden thrust the lantern inside, to be a tunnel of considerable length. This was the "Blue Room," as Harthoorn had called it, a new excavation, and a productive one. And since it was to this region that his employer had advised him to focus his attention, Warden wasted no time unpacking his tools and setting to work.

The task was a tedious one, and dirty, but not difficult. Where the tunnel was its widest, and highest, a small pickaxe was Warden's instrument of choice. The Room narrowed as it went, though, so that to work from one end to the other, Warden knew he would have to crouch, then kneel, switch from an axe to a spade, then crawl, and finally lie, arms extended, scratching at the brittle walls with nothing but a long fork-like instrument.

The fruits of Warden's industry, though—close to three hours of knocking clumps of clay and rock from the walls, and examining them with black fingers, straining one's eyes in the dim light—was a mere pair of small blue stones. He was happy to find even these, though; and retrieving a drawstring pouch from his front pocket, cautiously slipped them in.

It was tiresome work. He was tired, and needed rest. So Warden slouched down against the dirty wall, took a few drinks from his water jar, and gazing as he rested into the part of the tunnel just ahead, wondered if his luck there would be any better.

In the dim light, he could only make out a few small details. Here and there were bits of trash—an empty matchbook, a ceramic bowl broken in three, more than one rusted cup and, a little further down, a heap of rags that looked almost like the body of a man.

That *was* the body of a man.

Warden crept forward. The tunnel became so narrow, here, that it became necessary to crouch. Certainly, yes, a man's body—a lean man, and a tall, covered as much by dust as clothing. His eyes, wide open and still, seemed almost to look back at him.

"Hello," said the man, suddenly, at that moment.

"What?" Hearing, of course, but voicing surprise more than anything.

Except for his breathing—heavy, and full of dust—the man was silent.

"How long have you been down here?" asked Warden, at last.

The man was quiet a while.

"Three days." Silent a little longer, then adding softly— "Three hundred days." The man gave a low chuckle.

Warden looked over the man. Certainly, the leg was at an unnatural angle. The pants were stained about the knee.

"Are you—broken?" he asked, gently.

"I'm not broken," said the man. And then, "I'm broken. All over, I expect."

"In pain?"

The man showed his teeth.

"Can you move?"

The man nodded.

"I dragged myself. Back here. It was easy."

For a moment, Warden wasn't sure what to say.

"Can you guess why?" asked the man.

Before Warden could answer, the man had turned his head to one side, and stretching his neck, rubbed his tongue over the surface of a smooth stone, bearded with moisture, that jutted out of the dirt.

"I'll get you out of here."

"You won't."

It jolted him, at first, the answer. But it was a pessimism—common in cases of long or extreme suffering—that Warden had seen before, and recently, tending his father in his last months.

"What you'll do," said the man, heavily, "if you have any brains in your head, is go about your business. Is—" correcting himself, lifting a finger—"take my *own* stones first, and *then* go. There's a dozen here," tapping his pocket, "that I gathered on the first day, the morning, forgetting to empty them before going back in the afternoon. *He* knows. It's why he sent you. It's what he expects you to do. It's what *I* would do."

Ignoring him, "I think," said Warden, "that if I took you by the waist—there's nothing the matter with your hips?—I could drag you out to the lift—carefully—and then—"

"Get away from me." The man kicked at Warden, with his good leg, and a shout of—pain or hostility, Warden wasn't certain. "Just leave me."

"I *won't* leave you," said Warden, almost through his teeth.

"Let *go*," said the man, kicking first with his good, and then his injured leg, the scream of pain from the last shooting through the tunnel, a nerve, and up the hole.

Warden listened, this time, though not for his own sake. He crawled backwards, until there was room enough to sit upright.

"It's very simple," he said, breathing heavily. "*You* lie still, and *I* move you—down the tunnel," pointing back, "and then—"

"And then *what*? There's room enough, barely, on the lift, for one man. *I* can't stand. Not on my own. Not with help, even."

"We could try."

Shaking his head, "What's the good of it? If I *could* stand, even then, if we could squeeze ourselves both onto the platform, to make it to the surface, the balance, the *weight* must be just so, or we'd both fall. The board's thin. The rope. The knot would never hold." Grinning, "It's a long way down."

"Something could be done."

"By *who*?"

"Harthoorn."

The man only laughed.

"Even *if* he could," he went on, stopping Warden before he could speak, "if he *wished* to, he'd never have the strength, not at his age, to lift the two of us. And as for *help*," seeming to read Warden's mind, and stopping him once again, "the region's remote. And help—if help exists—is a long way off."

"Something could be done," Warden repeated, though with less energy.

The man again showed his teeth, the only clean part of him.

"You're stubborn as I am."

Warden rocked himself forwards, onto his hands and knees, crawling a few paces.

"Then let me help you," he said.

"You'll kill us both."

"Fair enough."

The man dropped his head back on the tunnel wall, exhaled loudly—and said nothing.

Dragging the man from the tunnel, the awkwardness in close quarters, the strain, was a difficult enough task, and one not lightened any by his screams, his lapses into resistance, the occasional kick. In time, though, the two of them cleared the mouth of the Blue Room, reaching the middle of the shaft floor, where the platform lay in a dim circle of light.

They rested a while, in silence. Then—

"Can you sit up?" asked Warden, at last.

"No," said the man. "I don't think so."

"You were sitting when I found you."

"I can't."

"Do it anyway."

With assistance from Warden, who held his shoulders, the man did, with a groan, sit up. Then Warden released him, checking that he could remain so independently—which the man did, though wincing, in pain.

"Good. The left leg—is that one good enough to stand on?"

"Hardly," said the man, after a heavy breath.

"Have you tried?"

The man only glared.

"Try it now."

He did—and roared.

"I won't do it. I've changed my mind. It's murder."

Without a word, Warden positioned himself behind the man, and grabbing him under his arms, lifted him upright, careful to shift the man's weight onto his good—or at least better—leg.

"Now grab the rope," he said, once the groaning and the dust had settled together. The rope and platform, both, were close enough, now, to be touched. "Grab the rope, and I'll help you on."

The man groaned—but obeyed, collapsing against Warden's chest, head on his shoulder, like a child.

"What now?" he rasped in Warden's ear.

"We wait. It's past eleven. Harthoorn will be back. Very soon."

"Who?"

"Harthoorn," said Warden, a little puzzled.

The man shook his head.

"He won't come back."

"He will. Any moment."

Five minutes passed. Another five.

"I don't know your name," said Warden, at last.

"Hmm? Warden."

"That's *my* name."

"Is it?" said the man.

"*Your* name. Tell me."

"My name," was all the man said, his eyes heavy. He'd lost, thought Warden, a great deal of blood. He thought of jostling him, but the man was in pain enough. They needed to hold still, besides.

The two of them waited, it seemed, forever. There was occasional talk—vague questions on Warden's part, always answered, it seemed to him, in riddles—but it rapidly grew more and more sparse, and lapsed, at last, into silence.

The man seemed to be falling asleep. He'd grown very heavy. Warden contemplated sitting down, or leaning against the wall of the shaft, even, when—

"Alright down there?" came a voice from above. A shadow blocked the circle of light, above.

"Yes," cried Warden. "I'm ready."

"On the platform?"

"I'm on it."

"Find anything?"

On Warden's shoulder, the man either laughed, or whimpered.

"I'm ready," was all Warden said.

"Alright," said the old man, backing away from the hole. "Hold on."

A long quivering of the rope. At last, though very slowly, it began to move.

"You're heavy," said Harthoorn, grunting.

"Fool," whispered the man. "Foolish. A fool. I was better, there."

"That's shit," said Warden.

"Better mine," said the man, breathing heavily, "than yours."

"How's it going up there?" cried Warden, still puzzling over the man's remark.

Harthoorn said nothing, but went on grunting, and grinding the handle.

They were ascending, Warden guessed, no faster than six feet per minute. It may have even been slower than that—and growing no faster.

There was a loud cry from above.

"I can't hold it! You're too heavy! I can't hold."

"You have no choice," said the head on Warden's shoulder, directly into his ear. "Don't give yourself grief. It's what I would've done. Believe me. Don't be afraid to."

With his free hand, the man reached down, retrieved something from his pocket, then stuffed it into Warden's.

"*No*," cried Warden.

The man showed his teeth.

"I can't hold!" cried Harthoorn, again.

The man relaxed his grip on the rope. It became difficult, now, to support him, to keep balanced. The platform began to tip.

"You're too heavy!"

Warden looked very closely into the man's eyes. There was light enough, now, to see them. His eyes—were so full of dust, Warden couldn't tell the color.

And then Warden let go of the man's waist.

A moment later, far below him, a soft thump, only.

Silence, after that.

Warden very quickly found his balance.

"Better," came the voice of Harthoorn, above, panting. "Much better. It's easy, now."

Warden held very still. In a minute, there would be sunlight on his hands, his face.

ANNA

She could be seen, Anna, fair weather or not, walking up and down streets that might've been bridges of vanilla wafer, so tentative were her steps. The straw hat, the woollen jacket—as characteristic as her grey eyes, her strong English chin.

She was not much to look at, no. And hardly what you'd call clever. Pardoned, though, at least in part, from the wrath of the public by the combo of old age and spinsterhood. People still talked, of course; but not as often or loudly as they might've. Which isn't to say she never *heard*. But knowing how tightly people clutch at their illusions, she never bothered to disillusion them.

Spinster. No doubt she hated the term. Unfair that when a woman remains unmarried, she becomes some sort of pitiful dishrag, whereas a bachelor—well, he's just *lucky*. Wise, even. But Anna—there was a good chance, anyway—was, if not clever, no, at least wiser than many cared to realize.

★

Fifty years earlier, her father had served as veterinarian, dentist, and doctor to the town's thousand-or-so residents. In no extraordinary day would he reach his hands into darkness and, some red-gloved magician, procure a colt, a tooth, a swollen appendix—and all before a light lunch of soda and biscuits.

Doctor Death, they called him, though not for a lack of success. The "death" part was a subjective, nervous term, as the man never administered anaesthesia in his life. This was purely on principle. "Now, stop your fussing," he'd say to one, in the midst of prying out a tricky wisdom tooth, or setting a broken limb, as though agony were a blemish of character.

When he died—not quite seventy, but one can only guess—the population did its best to crush into the Baptist Church, though the man was no Baptist, and never set foot in a church of any persuasion as far as anyone could tell. Dr. Hansen had few relations, fewer friends, so the larger number of those gathered must have been present, as Mrs. Hollier (something of a gossip) confirmed, "Just to make absolute sure."

Living as he did, retiringly, spending little on himself or anyone, the doctor was reputed—well, rich. A bit of gossip that proved true on the reading of the will, which left to Anna, an only child, on her marrying, his entire estate of close to a million dollars—a sum, in those days.

Reappraised, one of the plainer faces in town was now much more enticing. And it would be a lie to say that Anna, now in her mid-twenties, finding men other than the mail and milk variety on her doorstep for the first time, didn't enjoy the surplus of attention. Of course, the mail and milk variety continued to show up as well, but were twice as courteous as before. Which was nice as well.

Affection will settle, and hers landed comfortably on a young man—younger, about 20—by the name of Robert Allen.

Robert was not much to look at either. Nor particularly bright. His family, if reputable, was hardly affluent. Passing him on the street, one might remember, if anything, the practical non-existence of his upper lip. Or his odour, which, by no fault of his own (his parents were sausage-makers, and good ones at that), had a bias towards sage and garlic.

Of course, for several years prior, it had been no unusual thing for Robert to show up at her doorstep—at almost everyone's—in the capacity of delivery-boy for the family business. But when he began to put in an exclusive daily appearance at Anna's every afternoon at a punctual five-thirty, it became clear that she'd either grown unusually fond of sausage, or unusually fond of Robert. Public opinion settled on the latter.

For a time, café talk centred on the strangeness of the decision. There were, in the area, hundreds of men of better means, certainly better looks. No shortage, either, of more deserving cases—like Jensen the widower who, in the span of a year or two, had lost first his wife, then his livelihood. Why then this sagey Robert—heir to a steady, modest trade—who seemed nicely settled in life already?

They married the following June. Likewise, in the Baptist Church (it was thought uncivil to ask *why*). Likewise, as much of the population as could squeeze itself, stepsisters into glass footwear, squeezed itself into the pews. Though the abundance of Allens—so many sausages crammed into the front few rows—lent the small church, in the summer heat, an unfortunate odour, everything else went smoothly. "Both with and without a hitch," as Mrs. Hollier, who thought she was clever, noted, no doubt as often as she could. As the couple ran out of the church, half the children threw rice, half held their noses.

★

A month later, they separated.

Another month and Robert was dead.

To plot out the hows and whys is to draw on hearsay, guesswork, outright lies—a construct of cobwebs only. The truth of the matter was something that not even Mrs. Hollier, in all her omniscience, could divine.

The only definite facts are these. After the funeral—during which, it's said, Anna showed little emotion (but it was difficult, with the veil, to tell)—she turned hermit for a time, emerging briefly, over the next few months, only on a handful of occasions. And then, slowly, she resumed her usual routines and seemed, those who knew her best (not many, and not well) to be unchanged by the events of the previous months.

Nothing, in the short interval of their matrimony, had seemed to anyone amiss. Granted, one can't see through walls; but there are houses, well known in any town, where heated talk can be overheard at a hundred paces. There was none of that, however. No unpleasantness of any kind. The couple walked most afternoons, and seemed, to all who stopped and spoke to them, happy and in good spirits.

And then, four weeks into the marriage, at half-past five of a Friday afternoon, Robert strolled home after work to find the front door locked. No amount of pleading or persuasion could induce Anna to open it, nor could an explanation be procured. At last, exhausted, he returned to his family home, intending to stay a night or two, until whatever chance affront had offended his young wife was forgotten or forgiven.

And it was there that, on Wednesday of the following week, his habitual day off, Robert, his parents already busy at the shop, was awakened by knocking. He'd've likely ignored it, too—it was only just after nine—if the knocking hadn't had such a professional steadiness to it. Hastily dressing, opening the door, he was greeted by a severe older man in grey who presented him with a handful of papers, nodded, and turned on his heels.

Robert shuffled through them, one then another, in disbelief.

They were divorce papers.

★

The mental steadiness of the young man declined rapidly after that. By the end of the first week, he'd become sullen, untalkative. By the second, he'd given up washing, seldom leaving the house, and then only to bang, fruitlessly, on his marital door, or walk about aimlessly, eyes on his feet. There were doctor's visits, which became more and more frequent, and lengthy. There were whispers of hospitalization, insanity—a family trouble, it was said, for several generations. And when a failed attempt at his own life was followed, several weeks later, by one more successful, people were, if saddened, hardly surprised.

As for the sudden about-face in affection, there was, of course, no shortage of theories. Married life, perhaps, didn't suit a woman already accustomed to singledom. Some sexual inability on Robert's part, some suggested. Was there something—*unnatural*—about his new bride? Overwhelmingly, though, it was thought that Anna had no intention of remaining married to anyone. She wanted her inheritance—nothing more, or less. And this apparent coldness in a woman who thought nothing, it would seem, of crushing the hopes of a mere boy for mere gain, did nothing to earn her many sympathizers. In the weeks following Robert's death, public sentiment was so powerfully opposed to Anna that it was a wonder it didn't congeal, wield pitchforks, and drive the woman out of town. But small towns, and small-towners, aren't as medieval as they once were. If the public, for the next few months, was stiff in its manner towards her, it was a stiffness that gradually eased itself away and was forgotten.

A final theory. This one came years later, making its first appearance on the lips of some insignificant person, at the café, one afternoon.

"I was thinking," said the insignificant person, "about Miss Hanson." As she was the only Hanson in town, there was no need to clarify.

"Yes?"

"Well," pausing for coffee. "Supposing you or I were in the same situation—I mean in the position to inherit a bundle—but at the same time, not ready, or willing, to marry just yet."

"Mmm hmm," drinking.

"And let's say you or I decided—logical enough—on a quickie hitch-and-annulment. You couldn't very well let the man in on it. He'd only want his cut—and not a small one, at that."

"I suppose. Men are like that."

"So—if you were a thoughtful person, at least—wouldn't you choose someone who had something to fall back on? I mean, when it all went poof?"

"Poof? I suppose so."

"So instead of picking some hapless fellow, you pick someone like Robert, with the family business and everything—"

"Helen—" *(that* was her name).

"I mean, how could *she* have know he'd've gone off his rocker? Maybe it had nothing to do with it. There was his uncle—"

"Helen—"

"And his grandfather—"

"Helen—"

"And several cousins, too, that all—"

"Helen! I see your point, dear. It's an idea. We all have our theories. But I don't think it very likely, not in this case. There may be some doubts, a few things unanswered, true. But one thing, to me, is absolutely certain," emptying her cup, setting it down with a surplus of force. "The woman is a monster."

★

She could be seen, Anna, for the next fifty years, in her hat, her woollen coat, walking on wafers, first with a cane, a walker, then crawling, across pavement, to the churchyard, lying by her father, mother, not far from her one-time husband. And for all the contention, the talk, no fewer crowded themselves into the Baptist Church to pay their last regards than would've for the saintliest. Throughout the service, the burial, the afterwards tea— not a shadow of disrespect. If monster she was, the public had, apparently, long since forgiven her.

But people will forgive almost anything.

ETIQUETTE

Ev heaped the spoon with sugar, sunk it in her tea, then replaced it, dripping, in the bowl.

Joanne grimaced a little, despite herself. She was a *good hostess*, and a *good hostess* shows no displeasure at the conduct of a guest, not even if she's being unsanitary. But Joanne was fairly sure that Ev—who'd been staring, the last half-minute, at the tablecloth, and its pattern of grapes and cheese wheels (perhaps it *was* a bit loud)—hadn't noticed. So really, there was no harm done.

A few months earlier, Ev had experienced a "nervous breakdown," whatever that meant. Joanne had thumbed through a few psychology textbooks, but could find no mention of the phrase. After all, no one was ever diagnosed with a "nervous breakdown," as far as she'd ever heard. She'd a general idea it implied "went crazy," but was equally luckless, in her research, in finding anything under that heading.

Ev was a neighbour of Joanne's, had been for the past ten years. If they'd never been friends, exactly, they'd at least been on friendly terms—neighbourly waves, weather griping, and even, here and there, a piece of gossip shared guiltily, like cheesecake. But then one morning, quite out of the blue, an ambulance screamed into Ev's driveway. And Joanne—like the rest of the neighbours, no doubt—took her breakfast to the kitchen window and watched the hysterical woman being removed from her home, tied down to a gurney, and taken away—an unaccountable bit of business to Joanne. She'd talked to Ev only days earlier, and found her—aside from the mismatching socks, which she'd dismissed as carelessness—completely balanced and rational. Besides, nothing ever happened on King Street (named as it was after William Lyon Mackenzie, the dullest of all PMs). And yet there it was. So when Ev finally returned—in a taxi, this time, and far more tranquil a mood—and remained there for the better part of a month, without leaving, or having a single visitor, Joanne thought that she really ought to have the woman over for tea. It seemed the proper thing to do.

Ev lifted her cup, and took a sip; then, with a dissatisfied look, added another helping of sugar. This had been the third or fourth teaspoon in a not very large cup. Joanne wondered if there was anything *irregular* in this, or if, perhaps, the woman simply had a sweet tooth. She *had* eaten the better part of a plate of cookies, already—and her teeth had a distinctly false look to them.

The talk, so far, had been minimal—limited to tea, and which kinds they preferred, and how there was really nothing like it after a hard day's work. But that well dried up pretty quick, giving way to such a very long pause that Joanne felt something must be said, now, to keep things up. And since she couldn't think of anything better, she asked what civility alone had kept her from asking from the get go.

"So what *happened*?" she asked, leaning in, and looking as sympathetic as possible.

The question couldn't've been an unexpected one, but her guest, in the midst of dipping the last cookie in her tea, started enough to drop it directly in. Seeming to ignore the question, for the moment, she fished the cookie out, swallowed it, and wiped her hands dry on her pants. Then she leaned on her elbow, and sat there with her eyes closed, saying nothing. Joanne was about to repeat the question—she'd contemplated touching Ev's forearm, as a sign of quiet encouragement—when the latter, opening her eyes (but not lifting them) began to speak.

"I'm not a real person. I haven't been for a long time now.".

She seemed reluctant to continue. So Joanne touched her forearm after all, which proved effective.

"I was married, did you know? This was before I came to King Street. Happily married for more than . . . twenty years. Robert was a—tall man, I would say. Six one. Possibly six two. Closer, I think, to one," she decided, growing quiet again.

Joanne nodded thoughtfully. It was clear this was going to be a roundabout sort of explanation. But those are often the best kind.

"It was—around suppertime. It *was* suppertime. I called Robert, but there was no answer. Which wasn't unusual, when he was reading the paper. I called again. I walked into the living room. There he was, as I expected, with the paper in front of his nose, so I pulled it out of his hands. His *hands* stayed where they were, completely stiff. And his face—the *expression*—was purple," tapping the nearest tablecloth grape. "I knew he was dead." She rubbed her eyes, then her hands on the cloth. "I called an ambulance. It seemed they arrived before I hung up the phone, even. But it was too late. I knew it was too late.

"Things sort of fell apart after that. It got really bad, Joanne. It was especially bad for me, I think, having no one around. A strange family. *Estranged* family," she corrected herself. "And then . . ."

Straightening her posture, she drew a deep breath through the nose, exhaled slowly, and continued.

"I had a son. Did you—"

Joanne *didn't*. Odd, the way one could have a person live practically next door for ten years, and know nothing of them.

"He would've been twenty, or so, on his own, when I came here. An athlete, like his father. Very popular. He went boating, one weekend, up north, with friends. On the—what's the river?" squinting with reflection.

"Churchill?" guessed Joanne. That was one of only two rivers in the area that she knew the names of. Not being a very outdoorsy person.

"No, no, not that. It starts . . . with a G, I think."

"Gordon's?" Joanne tried, after a time. That was the other one.

"Gordon's River, yes." Then a sudden change in her aspect, as if a big cumulus had passed overhead, and left her wishing for a jacket. It was powerful enough, the effect, that Joanne instinctively folded her arms, and pressed them tightly against her body, as her friend continued, "It's a terrible thing to drown, Joanne. It's the *worst* thing."

Ev seemed, to judge from how still she'd become, and the fixedness of her stare, to require a little something in the way of support, here. So Joanne nodded several times, as empathetically as possible.

"And it was particularly hard," she continued, with the same dark severity, "the news, coming when it did, so soon after Robert, in such a bad place. So unprepared." She took another breath, drank the last of her tea, and added, "Then I lost my mind."

Joanne was very quiet. Because really, what does one say after that? And her confidence that she could grab the Emily Post down from the shelf, and skim through it for a proper conversational follow-up to *Then I lost my mind* was, for the first time, dismally low. So she said nothing and, embarrassed, waited for Ev to continue.

"I just—can't work. I haven't been able to work. Can't concentrate. I can't remember anything. Not even *faces*, sometimes, of people I knew. I just can't remember." She stared—not *into* her teacup but, as it seemed to Joanne, onto the surface of the dark liquid, penetrating no further.

"I'll be losing the house, soon."

Joanne found herself, at this point, withdrawing from the conversation—from listening, even. Ev's voice became fainter and far-off, then vanished altogether. Because this wasn't at all what Joanne had wanted to hear. *What* she'd wanted a nervous breakdown to entail was foggy even to herself. But it might've involved BRIEF NUDITY or RUNNING AMOK (something like that had happened, she was pretty sure, to an uncle) or temporarily confusing oneself for a French monarch, but coming out of it, in the end, quite refreshed. But this—was just painful.

"It means so much to me, Joanne, your listening."

The meeting had to end.

"Mmm hmm."

"So very few people," squeezing her hand, "*really* listen."

"Yes."

Definitely.

"You're a *good friend*, Joanne."

The good friend shut her eyes. Not to look TRULY TOUCHED (which she did anyway), but to buy a little thinking time. She weighed her options. A mock-remembrance might work—a dental appointment, a bus to catch—and then one had only to sweep her out the front door. It would have to be done with expert caution, though, not to appear insensitive. She wouldn't've cared as much a minute earlier; but after all that out-pour . . . It struck Joanne as disappointing that, despite *feeling* the same, and as determined to do something, it took only a pathetic cough, or a well-timed smile to change one's whole outward personality and behavior. Like when she was at the café, and thought of some vicious quip for the poky old waiter, when he finally came round, all she ended up saying, as he held out the pot, making a grave little face was, "It's no problem, really," and swallowed her bitterness and her coffee together. Joanne wondered if she was the only woman in the world who was continuously perverted into being a better person than she really was.

In the midst of her rumination, Joanne abruptly became aware that her neighbour, now completely silent and still, was staring at her with such a puzzled expression that she could interpret from it only that a question had been asked, and an answer was both expected and overdue. So this is what she said:

"Why don't you stay for supper, Ev, and we'll talk about it."

If this was a mispronunciation of "there's the door," there wasn't much that could be done about it now.

Of course the widow assented—if ever anyone's heart "leapt up," it was hers, at that moment. Joanne read more than gratitude in her expression, too, but a readiness to impose, as often and unseasonably as possible.

Which is just what happened. But what could Joanne say, after the fourth or fifth time she was drawn away from lunch by a tremulous redhead scratching at the door like a stray tabby? (She might've said plenty, of course, if it weren't for the initial slip-up.) And what could she do when the woman, coughing feebly, or fingering her crucifix, happened to let it drop that she was a trifle shy on her utility bill, but slip her the difference, and a soothing word or two, even if the *idea* of it, a minute later, made her absolutely sick? Or lend her an eggbeater, or a pair of stockings, as the circumstance dictated?

This kept on for the better part of a year, a tedious one, which ended with—a discovery.

Joanne had been baking that day—a Saturday ritual—and had enough leftover dough for an extra pie (a Famous Raspberry, as it happened). So she walked it over to Ev's, though it was a little over-hot, still; awfully hot, actually, and her knocking, as she passed the pie from one hand to the other, grew louder every second. But there was no answer—not atypical for Ev, who was often, for no good reason, too frightened to open the door (nervous people could be like that, Joanne had heard). So she let herself in. Desperate to find a spot to set down the hot dessert, Joanne raced into the kitchen and—well. There Ev was, dangling from—a wall-mounted plant-holder, of all things—the borrowed stockings wound tightly around her neck. This seemed an unnecessarily gruesome flourish to Joanne. She even dropped the pie, out of clumsy shock—and to waste a Famous Raspberry Pie, neighbours agreed afterwards, was a true sign of friendship and devotion.

Joanne really wasn't sure what to think of the whole affair. She was sure she'd done the *right thing*, even if the prospect had been, at least initially, unappealing. But ours is a world of exteriors, of judgment by action, only, and not of the moral jigsaw one fits together prior doing a good thing for a bad reason, or a bad thing for a good (thank goodness). Still, she wasn't satisfied, and sat for a long time after, thinking the affair over. Finally, lifting a hand to the bookshelf, she touched the worn familiar spine of the great *Book of Etiquette*, opened it up to page one, and began to read. The next time something like this happened, she wanted to be fully prepared.

14TH AVE.

It's hard, D. When you've lived a rough life. Gone through so much. When it gets better, D, even when it gets better, it sometimes gets better, you've still got—you remember. You just can't forget.

I lived on 14th Ave. A year, years ago. Just a year. I can't go there, D. I still can't. Walk by, even. I turn away. There was—I had a chance, last year, a job, on 14th, I needed the money, I really needed it. And I just couldn't do it, D. I couldn't. It sticks with you, D, the pain. It's always there. At your ear, reminding you. Speaking up.

You must think, I complain, D. But sometimes I talk just to remind myself I'm real. It's easy to feel—to lose your feeling. It's so easy.

But it can't last forever. I know it won't, forever. I hope. You can fight it, maybe. Do you think? I need to fight it. People tell me, try.

It isn't so easy.

D, I haven't felt right in my skin, my own skin, for a long time now. I remember . . . walking around, walking off the feeling, trying, when it first—when I felt it, coming on. I'd walk for hours. That was fighting, D. Maybe, that was desperation.

I think—I don't think I'm happier, now that I've stopped fighting. But it's easier. Accepting things. Even . . . if it means suffering. Not feeling it, the wind, when it goes by. Just laying back, D.

It's a strange night.

I Am a Butler

I am a butler. Though I have been retired for some time now. Once a butler, always a butler. A butler is a butler, is *born* so, even if he betrays his heart so far as to become a haberdasher, or a butcher. I heard my calling both early and distinctly, and must say I endeavoured to answer it with an equivalent amount of force and clarity.

From the youngest age, I wished to be a butler. There was no other vocation. My father was *not* a butler. He was a physician. As a physician, and a reputable one, he had difficulty—he had a very poor appreciation, my father, of my ambitions. His discouraging efforts began early, and lasted until, by way of permanently quitting his household, I sought out my first post.

A word or two, perhaps, should be said of my father. He was English, and though of only slightly more than standard height, counteracted the fact by having a tall *manner*. Add to this his cigar smoking (I only ever saw his face indistinctly, through mist), and habitual wearing of black, and my respect—which is only a ritualized kind of fear—for my father can be easily understood.

He was a man of strict principles, my father. When my behaviour was—less than decorous—he never hesitated to alert me, and speedily, of the fact. His preferred method was to sever from the willow tree that grew in the south-west corner of our front lawn, what is commonly referred to as a "switch." As is the custom with such instruments, he carefully stripped it of its subsidiary leaves and branches, and subsequently the bark (though this is less common), leaving only a smooth white rod of perhaps a yard and a half's length. This he would moisten with either water or beer—whichever was closest at hand—and apply to any or all of my back, backside, and hands, according to his whims,

or the perceived severity of my transgression. It stands as a testa-
ment to either my youthful rascality, or his own talent as a disci-
plinarian, that he seldom lay down the switch until large regions
of my flesh were almost wholly obliterated, and myself and the
adjacent walls very liberally coated with blood. The walls in the
cellar—for this was invariably the site of my castigation—were of
a dull brown color which, when speckled with blood, so strongly resembled toast spread with jam that it was only by focusing
on this humble commodity that I was able to endure these sessions, and walk away from them with my pride—and indeed my
faculties—intact.

Far worse, however, to my youthful sensibilities than the punishment, was the remedy—by which I mean the *treatment*. He was
a stern, though not a cruel man, my father, and if he inflicted an
injury, endeavoured always to heal it. After cleaning the wounds
with soap and water, he would retrieve from his famous black bag
a quantity both of hydrogen peroxide and cotton batting and proceed to sterilize the affected areas. To those familiar with the
burning action of hydrogen peroxide when applied to an open
wound, I need not stress the intense—if short-lived—discomfort
it caused me. In time, however, by creeping degrees, I learned to
endure the punishment, and the remedy, in perfect silence. I grew
accustomed to both; and do believe that, the last several times I
was subjected to them, I felt no pain—or at least no displeasure—
from either the falling of the switch, or the application of the
once-dreaded hydrogen peroxide.

It became my habit, after each of these trials, by way of conso-
lation once I had regained my mobility, to go noiselessly to the
kitchen, and prepare a thick slice of bread with jam. This I would
transport to my bedroom and devour, waiting for the agony in my
back (or hands, as the case may be) to subside, a procedure which
generally occupied anywhere from two to four-and-twenty hours.

Far from discouraging me, however, from my path, the suffer-
ings inflicted on me by my father served to prepare me, and well,
for my life's work. The hallmark of patience, the quiet endurance
of both tedium and insult, are to any butler worth his starch

absolute necessities. I attribute much of my early success, and lasting reputation, to his well-intentioned, if somewhat maniacal
energies.

2.

At the age of fifteen, I left my father's household. This early
departure was not, as he declared at the time, a sign either
of cowardice or incompliance, but a reflection of my own feeling of readiness to make my mark in the world, to take those
first critical, if tentative steps. I will *not* deceive you into thinking, however, that I went from boy to butler directly. On the
route to fulfillment, one seldom takes a step without breaking a
limb or, courtesy of some helpful creature met along the way,
having one broken *for* you. There is, in consequence, delay. The
anguish of delay is a greater pain still. That I achieved my ambition at an earlier age than those who stepped more warily
implies a capacity to proceed *through* pain—though not, it must
be added, without attendant injuries, both psychic and physical.

My first position was that of "green boy" at Tern Abbey, one
of several residences of the late Lord Winter. My role was, very
simply, to assist the gardening staff (or "green team," as they so
playfully dubbed themselves) as needed. And the need *was*, it
would appear, very great: on first being introduced to his
Lordship's assistant (who was responsible for all "hiring and fir-
ing"), he looked me up and down, shook my hand and, without
so much as a question on his part, or a word on mine, engaged
me on the spot.

He was a somewhat eccentric man, Lord Winter. A bachelor,
and fond of limes. He could eat whole limes as some would
apples, without hesitation, or the mildest grimace. As the only
fruit grown on the premises, however (though others, as his
appetites dictated, were delivered on a weekly basis), his Lordship
had no doubt long since grown immune to its infamous sourness,
as I myself became in time—the gardeners often dared me to taste
them—though never to the same extent.

I recollect being disappointed, initially, in Lord Winter. To my boyish fancy, the term "lord" conjured images of gallant manliness, of hunting and riding and the like. But there was little of the old feudal spirit in Lord Winter, or his household. Excepting short stay-overs at one of his other residences, none of which were very far removed from the present, he seldom travelled. Even more rarely did he receive visitors: the fruitmonger, and my father (in the capacity of doctor) were, I believe, the only regulars.

In truth, the only remarkable thing about Lord Winter was his presence—and here I refer not to the kind of personal ambiance that surrounds a man like a lampshade, but his mere *being there*, quietly watching, from the front steps of the Abbey or a chaise lounge, the comings and goings of the various grounds-people. In a long life, though I have made the acquaintance of many fine and distinguished gentlemen, the "image of a lord" that first springs to mind is always that of a bearded man sitting in silence, grinning on occasion, and persistently munching on limes.

I early on became aware of some kind of mystery in regards to Lord Winter's health. My father's visits became, over the course of my three years' employment, more and more frequent, to the point that, in the latter months of my service, a day hardly passed sans a medical consultation of one form or another. Though I on several occasions "ran into" my father, he never—though I remain confident he saw and recognized me distinctly—provided, by way of acknowledgment, a solitary word, or a nod even, in my direction; nor did he ever *personally* contact me again, in any form, from the day of my leaving until his death, some thirty years later. This is, certainly, to be regretted; but he was so disposed *against* my career choice, and I towards it, that nothing short of a complete reversal of thought on either part could have remedied the situation.

Lord Winter's chief oddity, however, was what I perceived to be a tremulousness, a *shyness* of unusual severity, and absolutely out of proportion to the circumstances. So great was his timidity that, in the course of their labours, if any of the garden staff were to come within a few yards of him as he sat observing, he would instantly spring to his feet and disappear into the Abbey, like an ecclesiastical rabbit, not emerging, oftentimes, until the following day.

The only man on the premises, it seemed, who did *not* provoke such eccentric behaviour in Lord Winter was his assistant, the man who had so recently and speedily taken me into his Lordship's employ. This was a Mr. Green, a man of about thirty years of age, who I understood to be a Frenchman. I will not pretend to have any fond memories of this gentleman; for a time, I lived in terror of him. He was a tall man, extraordinarily thin, and wore a thick, untidy beard that hung off his face like moss, and seemed in constant danger of dropping off altogether. As unsightly as it was, though, his motivation for sporting it was clear, as his cheeks and chin—one could tell from close up, only—were covered in spots and anomalies. Some of these were mere reddish bumps; others were more like sores or lesions, many of which had either been picked, or had burst open, and therefore leaked, and steadily, a clear, heavy liquid. If he became angry enough, and animated (which was very often), one could see that his tongue, which always made an appearance at such times, was not immune, either, to this mysterious condition. Indeed, it was so lumpish and disfigured as to resemble, I thought, a pickle. It always struck me as peculiar, with a doctor so frequently at hand for Lord Winter's sake, that Mr. Green never sought a consultation for *himself*: he was clearly a man whose health was declining, and rapidly.

The workers' quarters, unlike those of the domestics, were situated not in the Abbey itself, but behind it, in an unattached, oblong building. This consisted of a small central room, for eating and socializing, and a half-dozen small bedrooms, each containing four cots. I roomed with the younger workers, of whom I was, I believe, the eldest. Though we came from highly varied backgrounds, the boys and I (one of them was Norwegian), yet we had a single prominent thing in common: Mr. Green. That is to say, the *attentions* of Mr. Green. I found myself on the receiving end of these attentions for the first time about a week after my arrival, and in the middle of the night. I woke in great discomfort, scarcely able to draw a breath. A great weight, it seemed, was crushing my face into the pillow, an even greater my body against the bed. The pain was very great. My confusion, my mental turmoil, was just as severe. All efforts to free myself proving unfruitful—my own energies were only redoubled by those of my tormentor—I had no option but to remain still, to relax, and to wait for the event to pass. At no point during these attacks—which would occur intermittently throughout the entire period of my employ—did I ever see the face of the perpetrator; however, his identity was *not* especially challenging to determine. He was bearded, and fond of moistening the inner part of my ear with a tongue so coarse and bumpy as to resemble in texture a pickle.

Though I failed, at the time, to comprehend the nature of Mr. Green's attentions, believing them to be a style of French punishment, I in subsequent years came to recognize them as my own early introduction into the adult world of sex. Not a very auspicious introduction, I will admit, but an introduction nonetheless.

As could easily be imagined, my impulse the subsequent morning was to flee the place. Yet with nowhere to flee *to*—a return to my father's was out of the question, and there would be no guarantee that, leaving immediately, I could find work swiftly enough to keep the rain off my head—I determined for the time to remain, to steadfastly apply for any other work the news of which came my way, and to bide my time.

It was a month deep, perhaps, into this period of wait and application when there occurred an event so distressing as to alter my plans—indeed, the course of my life—entirely.

I and the other groundsmen were scattered throughout the lime grove on ladders, busily engaged in what, with the coming frost, would surely be the final gleaning of the season. I was reaching for a particularly plump specimen when my progress was arrested by a sharp application of pressure in the middle of my spine, the source of which proved, on looking over my shoulder, to be the bony index finger of Mr. Green.

"His Lordship," he said, coolly, "would like to see you now." Had it been His Majesty himself who desired my presence, I would have been less surprised, for I had never known Lord Winter to seek out the company of *anyone*—save, perhaps, as I noted, Mr. Green, or on occasion my father.

Descending the ladder in haste, I followed Mr. Green out of the grove and up the steps of the Abbey. He was about to open the front door when that piece of architecture beat him to the task, and out popped—my father.

I became disoriented. My legs, trembled. This was the closest we had been to one another since my departure. If he chose to ignore me now, when we were face to face (or face to fog, for a lit cigar, as always, protruded from his lips), then the other instances could *not* very well be overlooked as accidents.

I was about to mutter a greeting, yet something about his expression at that moment, as if he had just sunk his teeth into a lime, induced me to swallow my words, and remain silent. Our eyes locked. We were still, like rival animals. At last my father, taking the cigar into his fingers, curled his lips into a kind of sour half-grin of mysterious character. And then he moved through the smoke and in silence past me, down the hall, and out the door.

The room into which Mr. Green ushered me was, I found, neither office, den, nor bedroom, but some conjunction of the three. On the east side of the room, facing the window, was a writing table; on the west, a low and worn-looking sofa; and in between the two, lying on a bed of incredible thickness and luxury, his Lordship himself.

Closing the door behind us, Mr. Green took up a position beside the bed, on his Lordship's right side. I remained very close to the door, confessedly nervous, and eager to learn the purpose of this unusual summons.

"Will you have an apple?" his Lordship asked me, unexpectedly, gesturing to a wheeled cart on the west side of the bed, which was overburdened with a great variety of fruits.

"No thank-you, my Lord," I said, somewhat puzzled.

"Will *you*?" he inquired—of Mr. Green this time.

"Thank-you, my Lord, no," replied the gentleman, clumsily attempting a grin.

"A lime perhaps?" he asked us both then; and both of us, just as politely, declined.

There followed what is commonly referred to as a "blank space," during which no one spoke a word, or seemed sure of what to do. This particular pause was rendered all the more uncomfortable by its *duration*—lasting, I would estimate, some ten to fifteen minutes—and by the fact that his Lordship never for a moment took his eyes off me. As for Mr. Green, he could scarcely keep his eyes *open*, and wobbled back and forth on his feet, like one about to collapse from exhaustion.

Never has the urge to scream come so close to overpowering me as at that moment. I very likely would have surrendered to it, too, had Lord Winter not broken the silence, at last:

"I've . . . been . . . watching . . . *you*," he said, as if each word were a sentence unto itself. I was uncertain whether he was referring to his general habit of observing the staff (including myself), or the past several minutes of intense scrutiny. In either instance, the confession came as no revelation.

"A peach, orange, pear, plum, nectarine?" he then asked, in a louder voice, which had the effect of refreshing Mr. Green completely.

"I love them," said his Lordship. This was presumably in reference to fruits.

So began a second, though smaller period of silence, which terminated when Mr. Green, bending over the bed, whispered something into his Lordship's ear.

"What I wish to say," the latter began, continuing in the manner of one recollecting, with labour, the words of a speech, "is that I have been watching you. I have been watching you and in watching you have become . . . impressed about your behaviour." Here he looked questioningly up at Mr. Green, who gave an encouraging nod.

"And I have decided . . . would you like a plum?"

Before I had a chance to decline, Mr. Green cleared his throat.

"I believe that what my Lordship is attempting to say is that he's in need of a new valet, or personal attendant, having lacked one since the previous holder of the title . . . succumbed. To an enigmatic illness."

I could *not* very well fail to notice—though *could*, to understand—that Mr. Green punctuated the latter part of his statement first by looking askance at his employer, and then by rising, briefly, onto the points of his toes. Then the two of them stared at me with such keenness that I knew a reply was expected, and promptly.

"But . . . I thought *you* were his attendant?" I said, bewildered.

"*I* am his Lordship's *assistant*," replied Mr. Green, with severity, "*not* his attendant."

Though the distinction was not, at the time, clear to me, it was in hindsight an unfortunate and embarrassing display of naiveté on my part. I regret having said it, still.

"*Well?*" hissed his Lordship's assistant.

I must confess that, for a compound of reasons—my youthful inexperience, the strangeness of Lord Winter (who was presently burying his face into a grapefruit), and especially the presence of my nocturnal tormentor—I had never in my life felt so lost, so torn and so broken-down. I was very nearly on the verge of tears.

"*Well?*" Mr. Green repeated, with considerably more force.

"I . . . well . . . I'm—I'm not . . . it's . . . it's—"

"Just say 'yes,' silly!" laughed Lord Winter, his mouth full of fruit. "Say 'yes' . . . and then come and give me a kiss."

And there emerged from the lips of his Lordship a swollen, discoloured and lumpy tongue that resembled, in no small measure—a pickle.

Slowly, and with a feigned placidity, I backed away from the bed. My hands being clasped behind me, my intention was to inconspicuously grip the door handle, and to try it. My fingers fell on the handle's cold brass, turned it, and—

Locked.

"Don't. Even. *Think* about it," growled Mr. Green, lumbering towards me.

Retreating to the west side of the room, and wheeling the fruit cart between myself and my pursuer, I proceed to pelt the latter with various fruits.

"Yes! Yes! Yes!" shrieked Lord Winter, clapping his hands, and deriving, it seemed, a kind of childish pleasure from the spectacle.

As the smaller fruits proved—I will avoid a pun—not especially useful in deterring the Frenchman, I progressed to larger and larger ones, and succeeded so far as to push back my assailant to his original position, on the opposite side of the bed. The happy direction of a large, unripe pineapple directly into the man's temple succeeded in spinning him around, after which dizzying experience he collapsed onto all fours between the bed and the writing desk.

What followed was, I think, the greatest act of audacity in the whole of my career. Perceiving the window—which was considerably elevated from the floor—as my only means of escape, and taking advantage of Mr. Green's temporary incapacity, I leaped onto his Lordship's bed and, while concurrently dodging his hands and crushing his legs, took a flying leap onto his assistant's back. That portion of the gentleman serving very practically, if noisily, as a springboard, I achieved sufficient height to plant my feet onto the writing desk. From there, covering my face with my sleeves, I crashed through the window, and onto the Abbey lawn.

3.

The passage of time between my escape from the Abbey, and my subsequent discovery seems, in my recollection, to have occupied a matter of seconds, or perhaps minutes. In truth, however, several hours at least must have passed from the point that, rising from a pile of glass and bleeding in various places, I made my way, at a high rate of speed, through the orchard, across a field, and into my hiding place—one of the wooded areas that bordered his Lordship's domain.

It was here that—alternately pacing and pushing forward—I found myself overtaken, for the first time in my life, by a feeling very close to panic. At such times, the mind trespasses into territory it would normally, and wisely, avoid. The long shadows of the sycamores melting into the dusk, the *solitude*, and the rapid cooling off put me in mind of a boyhood camping trip with my father. This was in Bishop Wood . . . in Staffordshire. After we had set up camp—there was a tent for each of us, as my father, in his words, refused to "coddle me"—and got the fire going, my parent proceeded, in his characteristic, low monotone, to relate to me the story of the so-called "Wumpus"—a monster said partly to resemble a horse, and partly a hawk, or an eagle, and to haunt that very region after dark. This was complete with noisy imitations of the beast's cry, and the flapping of its wings, the chilling effect of which, on a child of some eight or nine years of age, I need hardly stress; nor should it surprise one to learn that, when it came time to retire, and to pass the night alone, in my own tent, I proceeded first to whimper, and then to tremble, from head to foot. My emotional state would, I think, in a majority of parental figures, have aroused pity, or some other tender emotion. In my father, however, such demonstrations provoked only annoyance, and attendant wrath. Ultimately, he consented to take me into his tent, though only after a suitable punishment—namely the holding, in silence, with my naked hand, of one of the still-glowing campfire coals, for a period of no less than five seconds. Compared to the unfathomable terrors of the Wumpus, however, this was an agony I was more than willing to endure.

It was in the midst of this reminiscence that I first became aware of what sounded like a far-off "woof"—to which, initially, I paid little attention. Dogs were, after all, common in those parts. I had more pressing concerns, besides: the encroaching darkness, the cold for which, dressed only in a bloodstained muslin shirt and coveralls, I was so poorly prepared. Over time, though, other sounds became audible—growling, panting, the snapping of a twig; and finally a high-pitched neighing so loud that, foolish as it may be, the half-formed image of a winged horse, however briefly, protruded into my terrified brain.

My anxiety now reached such a peak that, very like an animal myself, I began to run, to bound and stumble over logs and crash through branches, re-opening, in my careless haste, many of the glass wounds on my forearms and face. It was in this bloodied and tremulous state that, dodging a sycamore of unusual thickness, I found myself face to face—and even eye to eye—with a pair of deep black holes. These I shortly understood to be *nostrils*. There was a strident whinnying; a glistening of muscle, and fur; a ghostly rising of warm breath in the night air. And then everything went black.

4.

When I next opened my eyes, it was to find myself lying not in the middle of a dark wood, or even (supposing the whole thing to be a nightmare within a nightmare) back in my quarters at the Abbey, but in a brightly-lit and sparsely-furnished room. Besides the small bed in which I lay, the only other article of furniture present was a chair by the door, in which sat what I first mistook for a round-looking gentleman, but which on closer examination proved merely to be a woman of mannish appearance. Perceiving that I was conscious, and with the assistance of a cane, she rose to her feet and hobbled out of the room. My assumption was that she had been placed "on watch," and instructed, on my waking, to fetch her superior. It was while I waited for the latter to appear that I became aware of a pattering, such as only a child or a dog makes, in the adjacent hall. I was therefore unsurprised to see the door nudged open a moment later by a soft brown muzzle, which served as a prelude to a dog of unusual size, very like a Saint Bernard, though thinner, and with a scant coat. The creature seemed ready to pounce—whether in friendliness or malice I was not, at the time, certain—when its progress was arrested by a resounding holler of "Brutus!"

There appeared in the doorway a man of middle age, small in height though broad-featured, and resembling very much, on the whole, either a youthful, clean-shaven rendition of my father, or a more mature version of myself. It was more at the sight than the sound of the man that the dog halted, hung its head in dejection, and crept to a far corner of the room to lie down on the floor-boards.

"Hope he didn't scare you," laughed the man (and what a deep and a resounding laugh it was).

I shook my head. Though I was well aware that, in denying my fear, I was committing a deliberate falsehood, I have always remained a disciple of my late grandmother's adage: next to a falsehood spoken, a falsehood merely indicated is in *comparison* a half-truth.

"Now," said the man, sliding a chair up to the side of the bed, and proceeding in the manner of a doctor eager to impress the parent of an ailing child with the excellence of his bedside manner, "What was a lad like you doing in old man Winter's woods?"

"I might ask *you*, sir," I said, more than a little offended by his condescension, "the very same question."

"Hunting," was his brusque reply, delivered with a shrug of the shoulders.

"Are you aware, sir," I said, rather stiffly, "that you were therefore trespassing on the lands of Lord Winter, and that poaching is an offence against man, against nature, and above all against the Crown?" This may seem a strange utterance, yet— though fortunate and happy to have escaped what I could only consider, at the time, my *former* employer—something about my upbringing, and sense of municipal pride, revolted against the notion of trespassing.

"Pooh!" he cried, waving his hand. "*That* duck. Wouldn't know a poacher from a poached egg. No harm done, little man."

Although he was not, I remain convinced, entirely correct, I still had no interest in pressing the matter further. It would be more apropos, I felt at this early juncture, to express my gratitude rather than my petulance.

And so—surprising him more than a little, I think—I shook him by the hand, thanked him wholeheartedly, and extended my gratitude as well to his "person" (being unsure what to call the mannish servant who had since vanished) for watching over me during my unconscious period and, evidently, tending to my wounds, which had been both cleaned and bandaged.

"My person?" he laughed, with such ferocity that the dog— which I must say had an unusually nervous character—leaped a foot in the air, and dashed out of the room. "Hah!" he went on, wiping his eye. "You mean my *wife*?"

Though there was no mirror at hand in which the supposition might be tested, I am certain that, at that moment, I became very red.

"Don't worry about it lad, don't worry," he said, endeavouring with difficulty to supress any additional laughter. "No harm done. An earnest mistake. She's . . . a bundle of nerves. A simple mistake. Now," crossing his arms across his broad chest, and stretching out his legs, "perhaps you'll finally tell me what you were doing alone, at night, in the middle of the woods?"

And so, over the next several hours, I provided him with an account of my unfortunate life thus far. To my story he listened with real interest and, as instance dictated, many genuine tokens of pity, outrage, and amusement. Furthermore, he expressed himself so "tickled" by my precocious interest in butling that, coupled with his present lack of a domestic (the previous one having vanished under unusual circumstances), he was fully prepared, to my great pleasure and greater surprise, to offer me the post outright. His proposal I accepted instantly; and while my decision might easily be censured for its prematurity, still one must consider how tempting it was, in my condition of youthful eagerness and uncertain destiny, to accept any position (especially one answering a lifelong ambition) that fate so kindly waved in my direction.

"Excellent!" cried the man, shaking my hand, apparently just as pleased as myself with the arrangement. "And what's your name, then? Don't think you mentioned it."

"George, sir."

"Pleased to meet you, George," he said, taking my hand again.

"And what should I call *you*, sir?" I asked (for he had yet to mention *his* name, either).

"Duke," he answered.

Here my eyes became very wide, and must have provided such an open window to my thoughts—namely, a kind of awed pride at fancying myself the young butler of a duke—that my new employer corrected any such supposition, and quite succinctly, with a single volley of laughter.

"Not a *Duke* Duke, a Duke of anything in particular, you see. I just—I fancy the *name* Duke, is all. Though properly, it's Willard."

"Yes, sir," I said, bowing stiffly.

"Yes, *Duke*," he corrected, with a smile.

"Yes, Duke, sir," I said. This compromise must have amused him to no small extent, for had he not—in a gesture, I believe, of manly affection—just thrown an arm around my back, his subsequent eruption into laughter and attendant patellar weakness would have rendered independent standing, for the moment, difficult in the extreme.

"Come!" he said, after a period of recovery, slapping me on the upper portion of my back. "I'll give you the grand tour."

The "Cottage"—this was the rather modest title Duke had bestowed upon his rambling, 10-bedroom estate—was, by my estimate, more than triple the size of the Abbey, and as richly and elaborately decorated as any sultan's palace. There was scrimshaw, and there were paintings, it seemed, at every glance. There were even tapestries, which I in my innocence mistook, initially, for damp rugs hung up to dry. For all the opulence of his estate, however, the lifestyle of the man was simple in the extreme. He delighted in all rustic pursuits (hunting and fishing, in especial), and seldom if ever, though of a highly sanguine nature, invited guests of any kind. His was a simple and almost Spartan existence. Wife and dog seemed the only companionship he required—though even *this* interaction he kept to a minimum. While it is *not* my intention to suggest that there was no bond of affection between Duke and his wife, it must be noted that the bond was of a highly relaxed and threadlike character. They dined together, always; spoke but little; and each invariably became, it seemed, in the other's absence, substantially more at ease. As for Ulyana—this was the name of his wife—she struck me, much like Brutus, as a long-suffering animal, albeit one with no apparent source of distress. But such is the nature, I believe, of psychical ailments.

As far as personal accommodations went, I was provided, by way of butlery, with a moderate-sized ground-floor room of about the size and character of a child's bedroom; and though draughty in the winter months and stuffy in the warm, it nonetheless proved a more than adequate place to pass my evenings, as well as scattered unoccupied hours. The room was, while small in dimensions, *emotionally* vast; and I have never in my life felt gladder, or more at ease, than that first night when, as butler of The Cottage, I lay my head down and drifted to sleep.

5.

Life at the Cottage, for the next "year and pence," to borrow a favourite expression of my grandfather, continued in the same theme—i.e. one almost entirely without variation. If there is anything to be learned in the observation of men of a retiring disposition, it must be that they value above all else an easy daily routine, and derive as much enjoyment from its endless repetition as most men would the injection at regular intervals of small doses of variety. The habits of my employer were simple in the extreme. Each day began with a long and amiable breakfast, followed by a solitary ride, or walk, often for several hours at a stretch. While Duke observed, assiduously, the English custom of tea, his preference was to postpone it until *after* supper, taking the latter unusually early (at 4pm), the former uncommonly late (often not until 9 or 10); retiring always at midnight; and repeating the pattern each subsequent day.

Into this miniature culture of ritual, any variation in routine, however slight—like changes in a play, to the players—was bound to be noticed and felt by all parties. I will let this enigmatic remark serve as an introduction to a period of days referred to always by my imagination as "The Mysteries."

The Mysteries began, I believe, on a Wednesday. It was while serving breakfast—Duke enjoyed always a simple breakfast, usually either of toast, or egg, though *never* both—that, scanning the table, I noticed a curious *absence*.

"Is . . . one of the *chairs* missing, sir?" I asked. While there were ordinarily eight ornate black chairs around the dining table, there were now only seven, and these had been so re-spaced as to conceal the—theft or borrowing, I had yet to determine.

The reactions, to my remark, of husband and wife, could *not*, I believe, have been more at variance. Ulyana—one would think I had fired a shotgun—started nearly out of her seat, and proceeded to look more nervous and forlorn than ever. As for Duke, whose reflex struck me as the more sensible, he finished slathering a piece of wholemeal toast with black currant jam (I can be so certain because it was the only jam he fancied), looked casually upward, and remarked—

"Hmm? Oh, yes. Yes, I suppose one is. One *is* missing." And tossing a crust to Brutus—who so haunted the dining room in his canine dotage that Duke, moving in both bed and bowl, allowed the old beast to make a perfect doghouse of it—he declared his intention to "go riding," and excused himself from the table.

Nothing more was said on the subject; and though most of my energies were expended, over the next dozen hours, in tracking down the lost commodity, it was to no avail. It was therefore with a feeling of defeat that, the following morning, as I set down the toast platter, I had no option but to say—

"I have been unable, sir, I am afraid, to locate the chair."

"Hmm? What? Oh the chair. No matter, old boy," he said, slapping me on the back. "You *worry* too much. There's no shortage of *chairs*, believe me."

I continued setting the table, unable to shake the impression that something *else* in the room was now absent. It was only when I turned to throw a leftover slice of bread to the dog that I noticed that not only was old Brutus missing, but his bed and bowl were likewise nowhere to be seen.

"Has the *dog* vanished as well, sir?" I asked, now, with some alarm.

"The dog?" repeated my employer, brushing a blob of jam from his collar. "Ah, yes," (chewing). "Brutus. Passed away. In the night. Just fell down dead. Poor old boy."

"Dead, sir?" I gasped. Though in truth the dog was in appearance so very frail and unhealthy that, had it dropped at my feet and expired, it would have surprised me not one bit.

"He must have been very old?"

"Hmm? Oh I'd say fifteen, sixteen," looking to his wife for confirmation.

At this point Ulyana—more red-eyed and sullen that morning that usual—burst into tears.

"He was seven," she sobbed. "He was *seven*." And covering her face in her hands, she quit the room.

It should be noted that, whatever the fate of Brutus, neither Duke nor his wife breathed a word of the poor beast again.

★

One evening—an especially starry one, as I recollect—Duke and I were sitting on the second-floor veranda, with our tea, as was our custom. Ulyana, feeling ill (she was now constantly ill, it seemed), had excused herself. I was seated close to the railing, all the better for the view; while my employer, who professed a fear of heights owing to a childhood accident, was seated slightly to my rear. The night was, though warm, infested with biting insects, of which the black fly and the mosquito were, I believe, the principal

offenders. I had just finished swatting one of the latter when I felt
a second, sharp prick on the back of my neck. I cried aloud in pain,
and slapped the spot with considerable force. Turning to inquire of
my employer as to whether I had succeeded in "squashing the
bloodsucker" or not, I was surprised to see that gentleman in the
act of returning to his seat. On his face was a grin of the most
unusual character, and in his hands—a syringe.

And one by one, the stars went black.

6.

I awoke in a small, and dimly lit room. At first I was puzzled as
to where on earth I might be, as the furnishings—or lack thereof—bore little familial resemblance to Duke's flamboyant tastes.
Indeed, the only articles of furniture on hand were a solitary black
chair at the opposite end of the room, and the small bed onto
which, by means of a series of cords attaching my wrists and
ankles to the adjacent bedposts, I had been firmly secured.
Though I lay—completely divested of clothing, I might add—on
my stomach, still I was able, by craning my neck and staring into
a sizeable mirror on the wall just above me, to survey the room in
its entirety.

Via this mirror, I watched noiselessly enter the room a figure which, through height and bearing alone, I knew could be
none other than Duke. In his hand I perceived . . . a gleaming
object. This I understood, after a period of consideration, to be
a "hacksaw." I remember a sort of *vague uneasiness*—for a
moment, only—overtake me, a feeling which was swiftly sup-
planted by curiosity.

I resumed my observations. Without a word, my employer
approached the black chair that stood against the opposing wall.
In my initial survey of the space, I had made a note of the chair,
only; I now had the chance to examine it more carefully. It was a
dark ebony, most likely African blackwood. I now recognized it as
the chair that had vanished from the dining room some weeks
earlier.

Flipping the chair onto its side, then, and dropping onto his knees, Duke proceeded with diligence to saw off one of its long, black legs. Though I initially felt it must be a trick of the imagination, or at least an effect of the injection, the sawing appeared to be accompanied by a deep sobbing of a somewhat feminine character, as if the chair itself were objecting to the procedure. The sound faded quickly enough, however, and was soon forgotten.

Although I was, and very naturally, curious as to the purpose of this furniturial amputation—the chair was by all estimates an old and valuable one—still the ache in my neck had become so great that, however strong the temptation, I could no longer strain it by looking into the mirror.

It was while resting my head on the mattress (there was no pillow) that I became very suddenly aware of something cold, and very like wood in texture (though it was a difficult vantage from which to level a guess) applied first between my buttocks, and then, after a short duration, *beyond* it, slowly at first, and then with increasing amounts both of speed, and of force. Though my initial sensations were an alternation between cold shock, as of being abruptly splashed with ice water, and of burning shame, which so combined as to steam and muddle my senses entirely, this lapse of reason proved but temporary. I soon enough new *precisely* what was occurring.

Considering the thickness of the instrument, and the many spherical bulbs—some double the circumference of a cricket ball—ornamenting its great length, the process was not, there should be no need for me to stress, unpleasant in the extreme; though events of my recent history, annoying as they too were, allowed for a smoother process than otherwise, and a less dramatically painful one. I remain a devout believer in the principle that *everything* happens for a reason, even if that reason is known only by a higher Reasoning, one in whose divine Hands we must all at some juncture (which may as well be an early one) place our lives, and our destinies.

I cannot with certainty—my endurance lasted, perhaps, twenty minutes, before giving way to unconsciousness—say how much time was occupied by this initial episode; however, to judge from those subsequent sessions during which I remained increasingly alert, it likely lasted between two and three hours, including expurgation, and stitching.

Breakfast, the following morning was, I recollect, remarkable in several respects. To begin with, Ulyana was absent from the table—

"She's gone," explained my employer, "to visit relations. Her Aunt Jane. A remarkable cook, Jane. Pass the butter."

To my greater surprise, I was invited, in her stead, to sit and eat with Duke in the manner of a friend or equal, rather than to serve him. We said but little; indeed, he behaved much as if he had passed his evening reading a novel, or in some other quiet employment. When I stood to clear the table, however, he raised a hand to arrest me; and reaching into his pocket pulled out and lay in my hands—a fifty pound note.

The currents of the household, after that, resumed a more ordinary flow. While the incident in the dim room was, unfortunately, to repeat itself, each attack (though the term may be an unsuitable one, for I soon—to avoid the headache which invariably trod on the heals of the sedative—became a more or less willing participant) was accompanied by an increase in pay which, however moderate, over the course of some thirty years of employment, accumulated to such a point that I rapidly became, I suspected, at least as wealthy as my employer. Likewise his disposition—and his manner towards myself—during what could be called *regular* working hours became by degrees so mild, so helpful and benevolent, that I am sure many a guest—had Duke been inclined to receive any—would have been puzzled as to whom to offer his hand, and whom his jacket. And as far as Ulyana goes, the culinary prowess of Aunt Jane must have proved so very remarkable that she never, in all the long years of my service, felt tempted to return.

And so I stayed on at the Cottage for some thirty years. Though the episodes outlined above were painful in the extreme, still they were rare, occurring on average only once every six months; preferable, I found, to the treatment of either my father or the combined forces of Lord Winter and Mr. Green; and profitable in the extreme. So lucrative did they ultimately prove that I was able to retire at the age of 50—a rarity for most men, and especially, I believe, for butlers.

7.

The last ten years of my life have been spent traveling—to Thailand, Brazil, last year to Cuba—enjoying the fruits of as many of the world's cultures as time so generously permits. I have become, by my own admittance, a hedonist, and do *not*, unlike the majority of the unthinking public, consider it to be, in my or even in most instances, an immoral state of existence. An ordinary life is, after all, but a steady alternation of pain and pleasure. When the first half of one's existence, however, is completely devoid of enjoyment, one can be excused for seeking out nothing but pleasure for the remainder. The same ratio of pain to pleasure is, in each case, maintained. Hedonism is not so much an *excess* as an attempt, in a most uneven world, to attain *equilibrium*. It is a quest not for surplus, but for satisfaction.

Several years into this highly congenial mode of existence, and shortly after returning from a month-long sojourn in Hispaniola, I received an urgent missive declaring that my father was on the verge of death, and that a prompt return to my boyhood home, which remained his place of residence, would be advisable in the extreme. The rattling effect this communication had on my nervous system—the note struck the floor before I realized I had dropped it—was, I believe, three-fold. So much time had elapsed since our last meeting that I had forgotten—I had not even considered it possible, perhaps—that my father even *lived*. The prospect, as well, of returning to what was for many years the scene of my daily mortification and torment was not an especially pleasant one, particularly to a newly confirmed worshipper of Voluptas. Last of all was the genuine shock that any tenderly disposed individual would feel on

learning of the impending death of a close relation. I am somewhat ashamed to admit that, for a moment—a moment *only*, I
must stress—I considered disregarding the summons. And then
I threw on my hat and coat, and bolted out the door.

I was admitted by a severe-looking older woman—my father
had evidently acquired a domestic during the interval—who,
expressing great relief at my appearance, ushered me upstairs.

"What happened?" I asked, by way of preparation, when we
had neared the bedroom.

"I believe he's been shot, sir," she said.

I was silent; this was not the expected diagnosis.

"Are you *certain*?" I asked her, at last.

"Fairly. But you'd be the best judge of that, doctor."

"Doctor?" I asked, bewildered.

"You're not the doctor? Oh!" And she lay her hand on her
chest, by way of squeezing out a small chuckle. "*You* were quick-
er. Forgive me." And with a final, dry laugh, she pushed open the
bedroom door.

As white as death he lay there, on the bed, head propped up
on pillows, wearing only a pair of rust-stained trousers. It was distressing, certainly, to see the man who once figured so powerfully in my life and my imagination as a figure of strength and intim-
idation, sprawled now so pathetically before me. It was the first
time, as well, in my recollection, that I had ever seen his face sans
the obscuring influence of cigar smoke. It was a face . . . very like
my own face. My eyes moved again to the trousers. These were of
such an inferior make and material that I was both startled and
appalled to see them in his home, let alone on his person.

Spread over his bare flesh were two large bandages—one on
the centre of his chest, and the other on his abdomen.
Unpromising as these outward tokens of my father's condition
were, still I have always found that it is the eyes of a man, more so
than any other feature, that are the best indicators of health and
prognosis. His pewter eyes, however, I found so unusually dull and
tarnished in appearance that I began to sincerely doubt whether,
as I approached the foot of the bed, he was even sensible of my

presence; or perhaps seeing me, failed to recognize, in adult form, the unhappy child of so many years ago.

As I stood there, trying to determine which was the case, I became aware of a minor but definite motion in my father's left hand, which to this point had rested, perfectly still, at his side. This I watched him raise, by degrees—I suppose the whole process must have taken several minutes—to the bandage on his abdomen, which he proceeded, and with some difficulty, to remove.

I turned to alert the housekeeper, but found that—hoping no doubt to give us a moment of privacy—she had withdrawn from the room.

With few exceptions—there are always the idiots, and the deaf—quiet men are observant men. As a reticent and a watchful man, I had many years ago noticed in my fellow creatures a habit, bordering on perversion, not of *seeking out* shocking incidents or details but, when happening to be *at hand* when something grue-some or unruly presents itself, of being unable to remove oneself, or to refrain from looking.

It was in such a spirit that, though from boyhood squeamish in the extreme, I found my attentions wandering, however much I desired the contrary, towards the uncovered *wound*. Thankfully, that perforation proved nowhere near as gruesome as I had antic-ipated. It was but a small hole, perfectly round, in circumference approximate to that of an average man's index finger.

As I debated whether to reapply the bandage—becoming, in the process, I must confess, weak-kneed in the extreme—I again grew cognizant of a motion in my father's hand, and renewed my observation of that appendage as it traveled by near-invisible degrees to the bandage on his *chest*. This he removed with quan-tities of trouble and frustration almost pathetic to behold, yet uncovering, at last, a wound that, in size and appearance, was the exact duplicate of the one above his navel.

Despite my extreme reservation to mention what occurred *next*, I feel that, in the dual interests of veracity and of allowing you, dear reader, to experience the same satisfactory emotional conclusion to the father-son relationship as I was very shortly about to, I truly have no option but to continue.

For it was then that, in a gesture of unusual strength and velocity, he thrust said finger, my father, deep into the bullet hole on his chest. This triggered the release (*how*, precisely, I am unsure), from the exposed cavity in his abdomen, a minor fountain of blood, which vaulted both upwards and outwards in a single, high-pressure spurt, striking the lower portion of my forehead, my left eye and, most regrettably, entering my mouth, which had recently, and understandably, been expanded to the extreme. This unexpected occurrence so exacerbated the feebleness of my knees that I felt myself very swiftly sink to the floor and lose consciousness.

When I next opened my eyes, it was to find those of Mrs. Chaisty (this was, I discovered, the name of my father's domestic) gazing down at me, and at such a close proximity that, with the attendant shock, I very nearly "blacked out" once more. After a few inquiries as to my health, she explained that, on hearing a loud "whumping," she had rushed into the room, only to find me sprawled out on the floor. Her next course of action was to ask my father what had occurred. His response was twofold: to break into a grin of the most unusual character; and dropping his hand onto his chest, to expire. She had no sooner finished her account than there was a loud rapping at the door.

"*That'll* be the doc," she chuckled, rushing out.

After the funeral—if it can be called such, for Mrs. Chaisty and myself were the only attendants—I renewed, with twice my usual fervour, my quest for diversion and pleasure. Over the next 12 months I traveled, generally solo, though occasionally with a found companion, to Rome, Chile and Bangkok. At present I am anticipating, in the coming spring, a visit to India to partake of the healing waters of the Ganges (I have developed, of late, a tenacious skin condition). *Hedonist* I am, and *hedonist* will I remain, I am certain, until my very last breath.

My dream is to some day walk again.

THE RICHEST FUCKING OLD LADY IN TOWN

Now my husband was the druggist. *Thirty-one years.* Made more money, I think, than four-fifths—five-*sixths*—of the town. *Nine tenths*, maybe. He was probably the richest SOB in town. And when he dropped off, well—*I* was the richest *bitch* in town.

There's no point in being the richest old bitch in town. There really isn't. I mean, unless you let people *know* it. Every goddamn day. And Christ do I *ever*. I let them *know*.

There's this girl lives next door to me, a real screw-up, got knocked up three times by the same jackrabbit. *Three times.* No job. Just lives off my taxes, eating chips, getting fatter and fatter. Struts past my window twice a day, a stroller in each fist, dragging her tits behind her.

This one time her brat, the girl, the older girl, goes and kicks a *ball*, onto my lawn. My perfect summer lawn. So before she goes and tramps over it I dash outside, snag it, race back in. Lock the door.

Give it back, give it back, she starts bitching, jumping up and down, *on my lawn*.

So I crank open the window and I shout You fucking piece of welfare shit get the fuck off my fucking *lawn*.

No! Gimme my ball!

Off. Get—*off*.

No!

Get the hell off my lawn you worthless fucking welfare *cunt*.

I'm telling my mom!

Yeah? Well while you're at it, you little shit, tell her she's a—

But faster than you can say "slut," she runs off, the bitch, crying. *Unbelievable.* You pay for their heat and clothes and food and they roll it all into a lump and chew it up like cows and spit it in your goddamn face. If I had the strength, the time, I'd smash into their rent-controlled shit houses and choke the fucking *life* out of them. Every last one. Dig my fingernails in. They knew what to do with people like that in Auschwitz.

Of course, they don't have the decency to call it that anymore, welfare. It's "social assistance," or some BS. Everything needs a *ribbon* on it, these days. A *pretty little bow*. But where's the shame in that? Tell me? Where's the goddamn shame? *Social assistance*. Makes stealing sound like *self-improvement*. So they can strut back in forth in broad daylight, not working, piss-drunk, proud as cats, *improving* themselves.

Believe me, Agnes, there's a place in hell for people like that. There's a very special place.

Charles

1.

Charles. I'm so glad. Always, to see you, Charles. My hands. Just look at them. On the rail. Don't you think—I've always—they look like . . . walnuts. The hands of old women. Veined and grey. Wrinkled, and grey. They used to be . . . white. White, long fingers. Piano fingers, mother called them. Crab's legs. Those white crabs that move along the beach at night.

My hair is so light. Flyaway. The wind might take it away.

Take some. They're always, falling. In the wind. The cherries. They fall, when I sit, with tea, in my tea. No need for sugar. On my shoulder, they leave . . . stains.

Take as many as you like.

2.

Charles I'm so happy. You're back.

The heat. We're dripping, heat. Melting. Can you remember—I can hardly remember—a summer. So hot.

I am 92 years old, this year.

My father . . . was a doctor. Did you know that? He was the doctor for—fifty years. I helped him, with wounds. Deliveries. The young girls, so frightened, always. I could—better than my father, a gruff man, bearded, a large man dressed in black. Bluebeard. But they trusted me. Soothing. Smoothing their hair. They were trusting. Doves. Alone. And beautiful.

One summer. Hotter, than any other. Today, even. I recall. My first . . . patient. The girl was—pale. A doll. She was—white. Porcelain. There wasn't . . . blood enough. For colour. She was as cold, as white. The child, survived. There was death, and there was life, on a table. I saw them both. Many, many times, Charles.

3.

Hello again. Charles. We've been . . . friends, of late. We've been good friends.

They think . . . I'm a spinster. The old woman. Alone. No husband. That they can remember.

But I was married. To a young man. When I too was young. A handsome man. Once. He's . . . there. The lilacs. Underneath. Where he wanted to be. There was . . . romance, then. In death, even. There were roses.

4.

Charles. You comfort me. You don't . . . understand how. You comfort me.

This house is—hiding. The lawn. Willows, moss. It's difficult. Clearing it, away. Each week. Each day. Trimming. Too much. It's. The house could . . . disappear. Soon. Tomorrow.

But it's—paradise. Even . . . overgrown. It's.

I could stay here, forever.

I am 92 years old.

The cherries, they're as good, as they were. The first year.

Take as many as you like.

DREAMER

It's me again, D. It's been . . . a few days.

It's been a long time.

I was at the beach, again. Last night. A few nights, now. I got tired of walking. Lay back in the sand. Listening, the waves coming in.

I feel so humble sometimes, it's. Can you feel too humble, D.?

I've been living inside myself. When things aren't right, you kind of live . . . inside yourself. Nothing can touch you but your own skin. And whatever touches it, you can't feel it. It's not real.

What . . . do you do, D. When it dies. When your dream dies.

You're dreaming and you're suffering, and the dreaming keeps you going. But a dream gets beat up, D. It gets sick. And one day, you pick it up, and. It's limp. In your arms.

I don't think—there isn't a big enough hole in this world, D, to bury . . . your dream in. You wouldn't, if there was. You take it with you, like. An animal, that doesn't understand. Heavy, in your arms. Falling over.

I can't get past it, D. There's so many things that—you just can't get past them. There's parts of my life I don't ever want to think about again. Cuz it kills you. There's so much, D, that kills me.

I'm a young man.

Do you think, D, if I'd never had ambitions, I'd be happier, maybe? Not—disappointed. Just living, and taking what you get, and not hoping for anything. I think . . . that's how it is, isn't it. With people.

But I did hope, D. Real hard. And I can't—I know that people, they, when their dreams, they die, it happens to everyone. They go on. They're sad for a while, then. They put on their ties. They go to work. They work, and in time, they forget.

I can't do it. I just can't do it, D. When it's more than just day-dreaming, your dreaming, it's . . . blood. To some people. To me.

I'm in shock, D. I'm pale, and I'm in shock.

I used . . . to get mad. I used to get so angry. You don't watch someone, something you love, being mocked. Shoved around. I was still fighting, then, D. I fought hard. I fought so hard.

My dream's gone. It's gone.

I don't know what to do, D. What . . . would you do.

It's like dying. It's exactly like dying.

It feels like dying, D.

Just like dying.

PENNY FICTIONS

Mr. Penny's Poetry

As best he could recollect—though his memory, admittedly, wasn't what it used to be—Mr. Penny had never, in his life, been bored.

People around him, it seemed, complained constantly of boredom—which felt like a mistake to Mr. Penny. I mean, there are always so many things to look at. To consider. Sometimes, even . . . to taste. At the zoo, once, he'd heard a boy—he must've been a boy, though he was nearly as tall as Mr. Penny—complain that he was "bored to death." He'd said this, perched on his father's shoulders, overlooking the tiger pit, holding a vanilla ice-cream cone. Now, if Mr. Penny had only had a vanilla ice-cream cone (there wasn't money enough for that), he'd've been as eager and occupied as a man could possibly be—never mind the tigers.

Presently, for example, Mr. Penny was sitting in what most would consider a cramped, disinteresting piece of real estate—Room 15B of Hospital St. Claire's Emergency Ward. It wasn't, he was ready to admit, quite like he'd expected—there were no monitors and pumps and whirlwinds of lab coat activity (though some of the rooms he'd been ushered past were chockfull of that kind of thing)—still, there were a number of things to look at to hold one's attention. Like the fogged, sliding door that led—well, somewhere, presumably. The red cushioned seat in the corner. And then there was the bed on which he sat—not a very comfortable one, I'm afraid—thin and flat and hard. Perhaps he could ask for a softer one. With Blue Whale pillows. Those, Mr. Penny was convinced, were the very best kind.

Hours had passed since he'd arrived. Or was it minutes? Mr. Penny wasn't, as a general rule, very good at time-keeping. Or so people told him on an extremely regular basis.

Was someone going to come in? To see him now? He wasn't really sure. He'd never done this before.

Or had he?

After he'd looked the room over a few times, Mr. Penny knew that, to keep things fresh, he'd soon have to "invent something." Mr. Penny was particularly fond of his inventions, though it was difficult to put them into words. They were like—real cartoons. They could be animals, or faces, or just about anything. He'd imagine them in the room with him, sitting on his lap, or jumping from surface to surface. Furniture, after all, can only occupy a man's attention for so long; but his inventions *never* grew tiresome. Today, he'd invent a fox, with a straw hat, and perhaps a—

Wait. A cupboard. There was a small cupboard mounted on the wall behind him. He hadn't noticed it before. The inventions would just have to wait. The round black knob was cool to the touch.

Inside, there were stacks of—he wasn't really sure what. But they looked like—they *were*—masks. Like the kind doctors, and usually dentists, wear tied around their faces. Mr. Penny thought about trying one on; but before he had the chance, there was a pattering of feet outside the sliding door, and in came a short, dark-skinned man with glasses, a clipboard, and a black bag, who looked up just as Mr. Penny's hand (the cupboard was shut tight, now) dropped casually onto his lap.

"Alright," said the man, flipping through the papers on the board. Still reading, he dragged the cushioned seat over to the side of the bed—this was a little close, for Mr. Penny—and sat down.

"Penny's the name?" he asked, glancing up.

"Mmm hmm," said Mr. Penny.

"Good to meet you," said the man, extending his hand. "I'm Dr. Singh."

Mr. Penny stared at the man's hand. There wasn't any dirt under his nails that he could see. The fingers were very brown, but clean. So he shook them.

"And what seems to be the trouble today, Mr. Penny?" asked the doctor, smiling.

"My heart's not beating," said Mr. Penny, pressing his fingers against the side of his neck, just to double-check.

Dr. Singh raised his eyebrows—they really were, thought Mr. Penny, unusually large, dark, eyebrows—and . . . smiled.

"And what makes you say that?" said the doctor, gently.

It was Mr. Penny's turn to raise *his* eyebrows. But he couldn't really think of the right thing to say.

So the doctor opened up his black bag, took out his—was it a stethoscope?—and pressed it against Mr. Penny's chest.

"Mmm hmm, mmm hmm. That's about . . . a hundred and twenty," said Dr. Singh, looking at his watch.

Mr. Penny's eyes grew very wide. That sounded awfully expensive.

"A hundred and twenty *beats*," stressed the doctor. "Per minute."

"Ah," said Mr. Penny. And then, "Is that good?"

"It *is* a little quick, Mr. Penny."

Mr. Penny—though he often did—looked a bit confused.

"So it hasn't . . . stopped?" he said, at last.

"Decidedly not," said the doctor, looking over his glasses.

Mr. Penny shuddered. He'd had an aunty, a horrible woman, who used to do that—look over her glasses at him when she was angry, with her buttony eyes. She had a kind of trembling palsy, and he was so frightened of her, as a boy, that he sometimes shook nearly as bad at the sight of her as she did. She was fond of dogs, though, and had a—Mr. Penny wasn't sure if it was a terrier, or not. He generally called all small dogs terriers; though he was fairly certain this wasn't always the case.

"Maybe, you could . . . check . . . again?" suggested Mr. Penny.

"That," said the doctor, "won't be necessary."

Mr. Penny pressed his fingers against the side of his neck. *He* couldn't feel anything.

Perhaps, he thought, Dr. Singh was *wrong*. That sort of thing did happen. Wasn't it—it was Mrs. McMurchary, yes, who'd told him that . . . she'd gone to the doctor just last week, complaining of a sore ankle? And the doctor had looked her up and down, and said, "Ma'am, I'm afraid you have lupus." So she demanded to see another doctor—it was Ramshaw, the Englishman—who told her it was a sprain, that's all, and to "put it up" for a bit? That was a different *kind* of mistake, true. But still—a mistake. And wasn't the first doctor a—*foreign* kind of gentleman, as well?

Mr. Penny eyed Dr. Singh skeptically. The man had, in the meantime, retrieved a small rubber hammer from his black bag. "I'm just going to check your reflexes, now," he said.

Mr. Penny didn't like the sound of that. His eyes grew fairly large.

"Oh, don't worry," said the doctor. "Won't hurt a bit. I promise."

Mr. Penny was just old-fashioned enough to believe a promise counted for something. So he relaxed, a little.

And really, it wasn't so bad. The doctor tapped him twice, quickly, just below each knee. Though Mr. Penny hadn't *intended* to kick, he did so almost automatically, despite himself. Perhaps that was what was meant by "reflexes." No one, he was fairly certain, had tried this kind of thing on him before. Perhaps . . . he was a good doctor, after all.

"Hmm," said doctor Singh, raising his eyebrows again.

"Hmm?" reiterated Mr. Penny.

"Your reflexes," said the doctor, quizzically, "seem to be . . . *uneven.*"

Oh dear, thought Mr. Penny. Though he didn't quite understand.

"Let me just try again."

Ah. Mr. Penny saw what he meant, now: the left leg jerked just a little, but the right very nearly straightened, it kicked out so hard.

The doctor repeated the test several times.

"Is it . . . serious?" asked Mr. Penny.

"Well," the doctor squinted, "not necessarily. Just . . . it's just *unusual*, Mr. Penny."

"Oh." Mr. Penny couldn't see the big deal, then. There were lots of unusual things in this world. Wasn't someone always telling him that? Mrs. McMurchary, was it?

"Hmm . . ." said the doctor again. "We'll try something else. Turn around."

Mr. Penny moved his head.

"Your whole body."

"Oh."

"Now, I'm going to trace a letter on your back. With my finger, Mr. Penny. And I want you to tell me what letter you think it is."

Mr. Penny nodded. This sounded almost fun.

"I'm going to start now. Tell me if I'm pressing hard enough, Mr. Penny."

Actually, Mr. Penny found that he was pressing a good deal too hard, and that it wouldn't hurt the man to trim his fingernails a little more often. But he didn't say anything about *that*. He hadn't been told to.

"H," said Mr. Penny, confidently.

"I'm not done tracing yet," said the doctor.

Mr. Penny looked puzzled. He didn't see, after all, how that could matter.

"Well?" asked the doctor, a moment later.

"Umm . . ."

"The letter, Mr. Penny."

"I can't see it."

"The purpose, remember," said Dr. Singh, a little crossly, "is to *guess*."

"W," guessed Mr. Penny, promptly.

"It's nothing like a W," said the doctor. "Let's try again."

This time he traced a long, snaky pattern down the length of his patient's back. Mr. Penny burst out laughing. He was an unusually ticklish man—always had been—and this was an unusually ticklish gesture.

"Well?" said Dr. Singh.

But Mr. Penny hadn't finished laughing yet. When he finally *had*, he answered, "F. I think. Yes, F. Definitely."

Dr. Singh told Mr. Penny to turn back around. He did—and jumped a little. The doctor was staring at him in a very unusual way. Mr. Penny wondered when he'd stop—it's unnerving to be stared at, after all—and what on earth the man could be thinking. Because he certainly had a thinking kind of expression on his face.

The doctor shrugged his shoulders. Scribbling something on the clipboard, he said, with a sigh,

"Just have a nice day, Mr. Penny. Try to relax."

Dr. Singh rose, pushed the seat back across the room, and opened the sliding door. He was about to pull it shut behind him, when he chanced to look up and—

Mr. Penny, hands clasped, was still sitting there.

The doctor cleared his throat.

Mr. Penny only blinked at him.

Dr. Singh was about to say something—ask, perhaps, if he needed any help finding the exit—when Mr. Penny, pulling a folded-up sheet of paper out of his jacket pocket, said—

"May I read you a poem?"

"A what?" asked Dr. Singh, leaning forward, looking over his glasses, again.

"Poem. One of my poems. A new poem."

"Oh." He made a considering face.

So before he had a chance to say no, Mr. Penny unfolded the sheet, and began:

> *I'm happy as a humble bumblebee,*
> *As I've just had three apples instead of tea*
> *(I mean tea the drink). Mr. Penny.*

Then he refolded the paper, and tucked it carefully into his pocket.

There was a very long silence.

"Is there—more?" asked the doctor, at last.

"Umm . . . no," said Mr. Penny.

"I see," said the doctor. And then—"Just—just a moment."

Dr. Singh vanished, sliding the door shut behind him. In a minute he reappeared—with several other men, too.

They were all smiling.

Mr. Penny wondered if they liked poetry.

★

The new room was far more interesting. True, there was less in it—besides the bed, essentially nothing—but the two small windows, looking out onto a garden and a parking lot, respectively, gave a person plenty to gawk at. Mr. Penny was admiring what might've been a rabbit (his glasses had needed a change for a few years, now), when there was a knock on the door.

"Come in," said Mr. Penny.

"Come here," said the voice behind the door.

"Come in," repeated Mr. Penny.

"That isn't how it works," said the voice. "Come here."

So Mr. Penny hopped off the bed, and walked up to the door. He was surprised to see what appeared to be—what *was*—a tray of food, sliding through a kind of mail slot in the middle of the door.

"Take it," said the voice. Mr. Penny couldn't decide if it was a man's—a high man's—or a low woman's.

"Take it," repeated the very surly voice.

"Very well," said Mr. Penny, looking over the tray. Though it was warm, and smelled like food, the stuff on the tray didn't resemble anything *he'd* ever eaten. There were three rod-shaped things that had a fish odor, a kind of biscuit, and a few—he felt they were, most likely, cookies.

"There's no fork," said Mr. Penny.

"We can't give you that, sorry," said the voice. "Finger food."

Finger food. Mr. Penny repeated the phrase to himself a few times. But it still didn't sound very appetizing.

Mr. Penny carried the tray over to his bed and sat it on the bedspread. Then he slid the bed—it was surprisingly light—over to the window. There was no TV, and Mr. Penny was the sort of man who liked to have something to look at while he ate.

Outside, an ambulance flew out of—somewhere—and disappeared down the street, red lights flashing.

Someone, thought Mr. Penny, is having a heart attack.

Holding his breath, Mr. Penny pressed his fingers against his neck.

Nope. Nothing. Still, nothing.

Perhaps, thought Mr. Penny, I'm dead. This was something he hadn't considered before. He thought of it for a long while, between mouthfuls of fish, and biscuit. It wasn't impossible. Maybe . . . it was even likely?

Another ambulance, this one coming *up* the street, then dis- appearing—well, wherever it was they went.

Dead, thought Mr. Penny. Dead, dead, dead.

But no, he decided, at last. Not dead.

The food would be better.

Mr. Penny Meets Fernando

For some time—say, three weeks or so—Mr. Penny had been having trouble with his eyes. Not an *all the time* trouble, no, but—well, it started one day in March. Even after he put on his glasses that morning, things seemed so much fuzzier than usual that he wondered, at first, if he might still be dreaming. But no, Mr. Penny couldn't remember a dream ever being as fuzzy as that; he could barely make out the clock numbers, or the eyes of the three penguins and one cat arranged carefully around him on the bed. And it couldn't be a pill thing, either, since, after taking too many one time, and growing awfully drunk and dizzy, his neighbour, Mrs. Mickleson, had taken them away. After that she doled them out, one each morning only (which seemed awfully stingy to Mr. Penny).

"It must be an eye problem," he decided.

Eye problem or not, a man must eat. So he set about making his own breakfast, and the dog's (it hadn't come with a name, but it was a lop-eared dog, very long and quiet and red, like a sausage). This took a few minutes more than it usually did, and involved a lot more slopping and splashing, which Mrs. Mickleson was sure to scold him for when she came by—though his messiness, she'd told him, wasn't really his fault on account of his being so jiggly. Mr. Penny didn't know why, but his arms had always been a lot shakier than other people's, which made it very hard to drink coffee without screaming.

The blurriness vanished, thankfully, after a half-hour. Still, when Mrs. Mickleson came in to check on him, and give him his pill, he mentioned it to her—because she knew everything. She looked him over and said, "Mr. Penny, I think it's high time you got yourself a new pair of glasses."

At first, the suggestion had pleased him. It's fun, after all, getting new things. But then, well, he got to *considering*. He thought of how long he'd had the present pair (he wasn't really sure), how much he enjoyed the tortoise pattern on the arms, and the pride he had in the permanent groove that had gradually formed on each side of his nose where the frames dropped in place. They were very big glasses, and covered his very little eyes, which he'd never liked and were far too close together. But new ones might be nice as well. He thought about it for quite a while after Mickleson left. But he had so much important stuff to do that morning, like get the mail and walk the dog, that he forgot clean about the matter till a few weeks later, when he woke, again, with a bad case of "the fuzzies."

It lasted a few minutes, this time. Mr. Penny decided he'd go to the eye doctor right away, so he wouldn't forget. His thoughts had a tendency to wander from where he put them, or thaw and fall apart like snowmen and roll in various directions. He slipped on his long orange coat (Mr. Penny needed a new coat, too, only no one had told him), put the dog on its leash, and stepped out the door.

"Yes, you a pretty dumdums, aren't you?" Sometimes he called the dog "baby" or "pooch-pooch," or things like that, though he knew they weren't proper names. Some day, he'd try to think of one.

The pleasant thing about living in a small town (I'm sure it's been said before) is that everybody knows everybody. That's also the unpleasant thing, as Mr. Penny often remarked to himself. It's hard to do simple things like get the mail or buy milk without so-and-so popping out of a bush to say hi hello, or somebody (generally Mrs. McMurchary) crossing the street to stop you in your tracks, because she just *has* to tell you about her health, her dripping roof, her poor sick husband, and a hundred other things that no one could possibly care about. And there are so many old ladies who don't like to read or paint or knit so instead they get up on a stool and peep out the window all day, waiting for people to slip up, then kindly inform them (and perhaps several others) of the fact.

So when Mr. Penny and the lop-eared dog stepped outside that day, they both looked carefully left and right first, to be sure no one was coming. No one but Tompkins was around (poking through the trash), and he was alright because he was English and never said anything to anybody. The streets were still very mushy and slippery, so they walked with extra caution. The eye doctor was on the other side of town—about ten blocks—so it wouldn't be a tough trip if they were lucky.

Man and dog were just about to reach the first corner when someone (it was Mrs McMurchary) came out of the post office. Mr. Penny thought about turning back, *but that wouldn't look right, would it,* and held his ground. *It's too late, anyway.*

"How are you, Mr. Penny?" she asked.

He knew better than to answer. Mrs. McMurchary was one of those people who only starts a conversation so she can gag you with words and hold you hostage half the afternoon. *The more SHE talks the less you feel YOU can, and the whole thing is like having your tongue seized by a bird and slowly pulled out of your throat.* So Mr. Penny held his mouth tightly shut, and said nothing.

It didn't work this time, unfortunately. As the woman went on about her gassy husband, Mr. Penny looked sadly down at the lop-eared dog, and the dog looked back at him as comfortingly as a dreary little sausage of a dog can. A few times he threw in an "oh," or an "umm," but McMurchary's response was only to look up (and slightly to the left) and go on talking, which meant, as Mr. Penny had discovered, that the person wasn't listening to you, but thinking up new things to say.

At last, not wanting to dawdle any more, which Mrs. Mickleson always cautioned him about, Mr. Penny backed slowly out of the conversation, and kept backing up (the woman just went on talking) until he was on the other side of the street.

★

The eye doctor was a man by the name of Kelly—a cousin to Mr. Penny. He wasn't the sort of cousin who had a turned up nose and cross-looking eyebrows, or passed the time at family gatherings by pretending not to know one and eating all the good stuff (this was generally Mr. Penny's impression of cousins). Kelly was kind, performed his examinations with a soothing, mild voice, and when it was all over and it was time for the bill, always waved his hand and said, not smiling but in a smiling way, "No charge, no charge." Mr. Penny sometimes wondered how the man stayed in business; but there were always so many things to wonder about that he never dwelled on the thought for too long.

Kelly's office was full of people when he arrived. Mr. Penny recognized a few of them, but they weren't people he knew in a talk-talk way. There was Jo, the man who drove around town all day and kept the gas station in business single-handedly. Miss Owen the widow, who married only to get her inheritance, then killed her husband by knocking him off a ladder (or so people said) sat in the corner, flipping through a magazine. There was also a neat yellow clock on one wall that looked like a fried egg.

"Do you have an appointment?" asked the sharp-nosed woman behind the counter.

"No," said Mr. Penny, who went back to staring at the clock.

"You'll have to get one, then," said the woman, shuffling some papers.

"Can I get one here?"

"You can get one from home," said the woman, gruffly.

"Oh," said Mr. Penny, furrowing. "But I don't think I have any of those."

The sharp-nosed woman looked up. Another lady whispered something into her ear, after which the latter smiled and told Mr. Penny to have a seat. He did. It was really a very interesting clock.

"And how's Mr. Penny?" said Kelly, when he came out, smiling.

"*I'm* Mr. Penny," Mr. Penny replied.

The man couldn't have been in the mood for chitchat, for he leaped right into things. He had Mr. Penny look through all kinds of lenses and machines, touch pictures in books, and read the letters on the wall (that was always his favourite part). Mr. Penny told him about the blurriness, and Kelly said there wasn't anything the matter with his eyes, and he could keep the old glasses if he liked. Mr. Penny was glad to hear it.

"But I'll send you for one more test," smiled Kelly, "just to be sure."

"Alright," said Mr. Penny.

★

A few weeks later, Mrs. Mickleson drove him to Outbridge, a city to the north where Mr. Penny had been once or twice as a boy. They went into a small room in a big building, and waited there half the day. Mickleson didn't seem to mind. When there were other people in the room, she chatted to them (sometimes in a very low voice), and when there weren't she pulled some knitting out her bag, and worked on that. Mr. Penny sometimes wished he had knitting to work on; he was never sure what to do with his hands. He tried doing the church and steeple, but it never worked out right (and who doesn't get tired of that, after a few rounds?). There was really nothing for him to do, or even to look at. No clocks or anything, just a small room full of nervous faces.

Someone (a young, pretty girl) finally called him and, Mickleson staying behind, took him to a larger room—the "testing room," she called it. This time there were no books to touch or letters to read, just a giant machine that swallowed Mr. Penny right up, made some awful buzzing and whirring sounds, then spat him back out. It was frightening, to be sure, but over soon enough. The same girl took him back to the same small room, where Mrs. Mickleson was whooping it up with a lady in a sling.

Mr. Penny sat down, leaned on one arm, then the other, and fell asleep.

★

"I'm very sorry to tell you, sir," said the big bearded doctor, in a serious doctor voice, "that you have a tumour."

"I don't understand."

"Well . . . it's a thing that's growing inside of your head."

"Like a mushroom?" asked Mr. Penny.

"Well . . . not quite. It's not a *plant*, no. It's more like—"

"An animal?"

"Hmm . . ." The doctor squeezed his eyebrows together, which Mr. Penny knew meant that he was *considering* something.

"What kind of animal is it? What's it like? I enjoy dogs and also rabbits."

The doctor went on considering.

★

The next few days were, Mr. Penny thought, among the best in his life. Mrs. Mickleson was unusually kind to him, and let him have all sorts of new pills. Instead of yakking to him in the streets, Mrs. McMurchary would smile sadly, and pass with only a nod. He was even invited to dinner by his cousins, who surprised Mr. Penny by talking to him like a friend, and letting him have as much of the "good stuff" as he pleased.

One afternoon, on the way home from one of these dinners, Mr. Penny came down with a serious case of "the luckies," as he liked to call it. To begin with, he wasn't stopped by anybody, though there were several close calls (more than once, he had to duck behind a telephone pole, or a streetlamp). And then, a block from home, he found a bit of treasure on the ground. It wasn't a big time treasure, no, but—well, it was a matchbook. "Guy and Fer-nan-do," he said, sounding out the words on the back. "At-torn-eys. Off-ice hours. Ten to four. Hmm . . ." And he stuffed it into the pocket of his orange coat.

Later on, when he was dressing for afternoon walk time, Mr. Penny pulled the matchbox out of his coat pocket, and squinted at it.

"Dog," he said. The dog looked up at him. "You'll be Guy." The dog gave a considering look, and then a resigned one.

"And *you*," he said, pointing to his forehead—"you'll be Fer-nan-do."

He opened the door.

"No," he said to the dog. "Just Fernando, today."

The dog looked skeptical, then pouty, then lay down in its basket.

Mr. Penny and Fernando stepped outside. It was, after all, a beautiful day.

Mr. Penny Speaks Up

"Whose is it?"

It had taken the man a long time to ask. One doesn't sit next to a stranger, least of all at the graveside service of another unknown, without going through certain silent pleasantries, like adjusting one's hat, and clearing one's throat, and crossing and uncrossing one's legs several times. Artie had been en route to laying a fresh batch of roses (fake) on his wife's grave—he did it every five years or so—when he'd noticed the spectacle. Not that a casket and clergyman are out of place in a graveyard, but for only one of fifty or so neatly arranged mourners' seats to be occupied, and that by a man struggling to keep a Siamese cat from bounding off his lap—well. Though his memory had begun to fail him in recent years, Artie couldn't recollect seeing anything so droll as that, not in a long time, and so couldn't resist stopping. Besides, he was easily bored, and marital duties are easily boring. The question, even after the courtesies, bordered on rudeness, perhaps; but Artie was OK with that.

"Mavor," replied the man, stroking the cat.

"*The first breath is the beginning of death.*" (This was the clergyman talking).

"Ah," said Artie. And after the required pause, "Mavor who?"

"I'm waiting to find out."

"*Life itself is but the shadow of death, and souls but the shadows of the living.*"

"You mean you don't know?"

The man with the cat looked puzzled. "Why should I?"

"Ha! So we *both* sat down out of goddamned curiosity?"

"I sat down," the man said, stroking the cat, "because my feet hurt. These aren't my new shoes yet. I need special shoes, and I'm waiting for them to come. They're black shoes with a special arch. God didn't make my feet right. This happens sometimes. It's nothing to get upset about. These brown ones are all worn out. It hurts to walk in them, but a man must walk."

"True, true," said Artie, with a mild, knowing smile.

"Also, I enjoy stories. These men tell good stories."

"*And the sea gave up the dead which were in it; and death and Hell delivered up the dead which were in them: and they were judged every man according to his works.*"

"Right," Artie chuckled. "I'll bet he's a real smash at parties."

"Hmm?"

"Never mind." Artie crossed and uncrossed his legs, then ventured another question. "So's he said anything particular about the stiff?"

"Stiff?"

"Our man in the casket. Mavor, was it?"

"*For all flesh is as grass, and all the glory of man as the flower of grass. The grass withereth, and the flower thereof falleth away.*"

"Ummm. No. But a few things, yes. Seems they hung him . . . on a cross, and he died that way. For our sins, I think it was. Sounds just *awful.*"

In a second, Artie's mouth rippled from a grin to a grimace to that same mild, knowing smile.

"*He that is today a king tomorrow shall die.*"

"No doubt," said Artie. Then after a while, waving the bunch of roses as he spoke, "But aren't you curious how a man can live that many years, and not a single person shows up for his funeral—I mean, besides you and I?"

"Hmm. No, puss!" The cat, making a sudden leap, was barely stopped with a dexterous pretzel of a choke hold. It growled, tail swishing, as its captor went on, "Umm. Well, I hardly know anybody. Probably Mrs. Mickleson will come to mine, if she's still alive. She lives across from me. She's 76. I'm 33."

"Not very likely, I'm afraid."

"Well, I might die soon."

"We can always hope for that. Ha! A little joke—don't look so offended."

"Oh."

"Though you might have reason to be. I hope you're not ill?"

"Ill? No." A substantial pause between the words.

"And not planning to leap off a bridge or rooftop any time soon?"

"Why would I do that?"

"Right, right."

A long quiet.

"Lord knows I'm not as kind as I could be, but I'd like to think I'm not such a badger that nobody, not a damned soul, would take the time to see me off. The name's Artie, by the way."

"Oh."

"And yours is?"

"Penny."

"Your name is Penny?"

"Mr."

"Mr. Penny?"

"Ummm . . . right."

"*For we brought nothing into this world, and it is certain we carry nothing out.*"

"Right. Well—Mr. Penny—it's just sad, that's all. No children, grandchildren, nothing. Likely died alone. Can't've been a rich man."

"Why's that?"

"Didn't you just hear the preacher? 'He was rich in spirit.' Spirit—this is what the poor have to content themselves with. 'Darling, could you pass the ham?' 'Ham? Dearest, there isn't any. We can't afford it.' 'Oh. Well, in that case I'll settle for some spirit.' *Spirits*, maybe. The hard-up turn to the hard stuff pretty readily." Leaning back, appraisingly, "Poor, certainly. Average-looking casket. And—this is the giveaway—no mourners. Not even a long lost cousin, hoping for a slice of the pie."

"I don't see any pie."

" 'There isn't any, said the March Hare.' Ha! Ever read that one, as a—child?"

Mr. Penny looked puzzled.

"Forget it." Smiling, "What's with the cat, by the way?"

"I'm not sure what you mean."

"The lump of fur clawing your lap."

"Oh—I'm not sure. I don't have a cat, I have a dog. This cat is a Siamese cat. A Siamese cat is called a Siamese because—well, I can't remember. It came to me as I sat, and rubbed against my leg, so I captured it. I'm very kind to animals."

"I think the cat might disagree," judging by the growling. "Now, don't look offended. You can't take a joke can you, Mr. Penny?"

"I don't like to be made fun of."

"I wasn't making fun."

"*And immediately the angel of the Lord smote him, because he gave not God the glory: and he was eaten of worms, and gave up the ghost.*"

"Do you think," said Mr. Penny, in a small voice, "the ghost is *inside*," gesturing to the coffin.

"Ha! Well, you never know. We could always open the casket a crack, and find out. How about it?"

"Ummm . . . no. No thank-you," squeezing the cat very hard.

"I'm only teasing, Mr. Penny. Oh—sorry."

"*Amen.*" And muttering something about last respects, the clergyman snapped his Bible shut, and wandered off. After reaching a respectable distance, he paused, lit a cigarette, and continued on his way.

"I believe in God, personally," Artie said, crossing his arms. "You?"

"Ummm . . . I've never really thought about it."

"Come *on*. Really?"

"Mmm hmm."

"I've always believed in a God. Not really in a Christian sense, but a higher power. Better to think *everything* came from *something,* or *someone*—more logical, too—than that it just always existed. 'It expands! It contracts! It's the *Magic Putty Universe*,' our men of science cry. Well, *I* cry back, 'And where the *hell* did it come from? Tell me—or shut up!' Ha!"

This was where Mr. Penny began to sink in his chair a little. He knew this kind of man. He wasn't the kind of old man who talks to you for a bit about weather or politics or something, then wanders off to feed the birds. This kind of man always knew lots of things that Mr. Penny didn't understand, and that most people don't like to hear about. Mr. Penny knew he was quiet (everyone told him so), and this kind of man took advantage of it, like Mrs. Mickleson said, by dumping all the nutty ideas he's piled up in his head over the years, like a prudent squirrel, knowing quiet people won't interrupt. Mrs. Mickleson had advised him to just get up and walk away when people like this bothered him. Mr. Penny thought this was a very good idea—but it was awfully hard to do when you'd been talking to a person for a while, and they seemed kind, and you could remember the colour of their eyes even when you looked away. So Mr. Penny waited patiently for him to finish.

"Still, I was a bit like you, I guess. I never gave it much thought. Too busy. After I retired—owned a camera shop, never missed a day—I had plenty of time for thinking, though. Reflected on all the awful things, wars and illnesses, that my generation has lived through. Train wrecks, gas chambers, fire ovens— you know, real cheerful stuff. Came to the conclusion that God was either indifferent—which is bad—or pure demonic evil— which is worse. I'm afraid I settled on the latter."

Mr. Penny, sinking a bit further, began to grind his teeth.

"And so I went on thinking, 'If God is demonic evil, honouring that evil is a perversion. Religion is satanic.' I thought a long while about what the purpose, if any, of our existence might be, about our high-pressure world of technology and progress. Do you know what I came up with?"

Mr. Penny shook his head, grinding harder. He knew that, by this point, the man didn't even care if he was listening, or if he understood a word. He was enjoying the luxury of talking to himself without looking insane.

"The purpose of existence is (are you ready?) *to kill God*. Not metaphysically, not in an abstract sense, but in the flesh. I believe that all our technology, our science of rockets and atoms and telescopes and such will eventually—in a million years, perhaps—lead us directly to God, busy creating and destroying like a temperamental child with a set of blocks in some far-off corner of the universe. This great confrontation is the purpose of our existence, is human destiny. We might not succeed. Others, after all, might have attempted before us, and failed. But if we do succeed (I have great confidence in the human race) we would *become* God. It would be the end of all suffering and fatality. All of creation would be ours to recreate, to rule over; to destroy, if necessary. It would be wonderful."

Mr. Penny, by this point, had sunk as far down in the chair as he possibly could. His complexion had become very red. Artie had just curled his lips into a particularly satisfied grin (which meant he was about to speak), when Mr. Penny, dropping the cat, sprang to his feet. Before Artie even had the chance to look astonished, Mr. Penny had both hands tightly around the man's neck.

Under ordinary circumstances, Mr. Penny wasn't one to speak up. This wasn't one of those circumstances. Shaking the man, who was really very small in comparison, Mr. Penny spoke up. Loudly.

"Why do you tell this to me?" he cried. "I don't want to hear it. I know you and I don't like you. Your wife would slap you if you told her what you told me. Your friends would kick you in the teeth. Are you crazy? Does it make you happy to make me sad? Do you go around hunting for soft-looking people, quiet-seeming people? I won't be one of them. What's the point of thinking these things? What's the point of saying them? I don't know anything about God. I don't think God is terrible. You're a comfortable man, I can tell. Can you afford to be unhappy? *I* can't. You've lived a long time. A good life, I bet. Lots of friends. But you pucker your mouth up. You lift your nose, like the whole world's just . . . one big—smelly—*turd*. You stupid, ungrateful baby. I think you're the devil."

The man suddenly became very floppy, and heavy. Mr. Penny let him sink to the ground.

"*Now* look what you've done. *Now* look. And the cat's gone, too. You frightened him. This is . . . just . . . *awful.*"

With a final shout, Mr. Penny staggered away, rubbing his eyes. But then he stopped, and backtracking a few paces, retrieved the bunch of roses Artie, defending his life, had dropped onto his seat. Mr. Penny smelled them. Though they were obvious plastic fakes, he looked genuinely pleased, and quit his sobbing—like the temperamental boy who got the chocolate bar in the end. And off he went.

Mr. Penny's Experiment

Lately, Mr. Penny hadn't been feeling well, not by a long shot. He didn't have a cough or a headache or a sore throat—nothing like that. But he felt so glum and sleepy in general that he spent day after day slouching on the chesterfield, and sometimes didn't bother getting out of bed at all. When Mrs. Mickleson (from across the hall) was still home, she'd taken his temperature and looked at his tongue, but said nothing was wrong with him, that it was only the "blue devils." Though she'd explained what the expression meant (Mr. Penny had looked more confused than usual), he still wished she'd found another way of saying it. "Blue devils" made him think of horned things bounding around his skull. "Take it easy for a few days, Mr. Penny," she'd told him, "and you'll be fit as a fiddle. Just wait. By the time I get back from Ireland, you'll be a new man." At the time, she'd been preparing for a long-hoped-for trip to Dublin, to visit her sister. Though Mrs. Mickleson was reluctant to leave Mr. Penny—she'd mothered him for the past ten years, at least, and he did seem to be in a bad way—she'd already purchased her ticket; she and her sister were getting on in years; and besides, Mr. Penny would almost certainly be fine on his own for a few weeks. So she did what she could to comfort him, made him a big pot of soup, even, and reminded him to take his medicine every morning. "A little of my beet soup, Mr. Penny, and you'll feel better in no time."

This wasn't the case, unfortunately. His friend had been gone for a week now, and though Mr. Penny had taken the soup liberally, he felt worse than ever. Now his head *did* ache. His appetite left him. If it hadn't been for Guy, his dachshund—he needed to be let out, of course—or to use the toilet himself, he wouldn't have stirred from his bed at all. He grew thinner, and ragged-looking, but wouldn't have realized if he hadn't glanced in the bathroom mirror, once, in passing. After that, he avoided shiny surfaces altogether.

He didn't sleep, exactly, but lay there all day and night, very still. To pass the time, at first, he imagined he was an Eskimo, hiding from polar bears in a dome of bedspread and sheet. But when he started hoping the bears would hurry up already and break in, he decided it was best to think of something else. For a long while he pretended—or was it really the case (it was getting hard to tell)—that there was a small boy in the pit of his stomach, sitting on a lump of something, and dangling his feet in the water. "What are you going to do?" the boy would ask him, from time to time. But Mr. Penny could never think of a satisfactory answer.

By the eighth morning, he found himself practically unable to think. He forgot about the boy, the bears, even the dog, which spent most of the day whimpering at the side of the bed. So Mr. Penny passed the time by *looking* at things. The armchair; the lamp, which had been on for several days and nights now; drawings he'd tacked onto the wall. And a picture. Not a photograph, no, and not a painting, but something he'd clipped out of a magazine, once, and put in a frame that Mrs. Mickleson had given to him. It was a picture, an etching of an angel—or. Mr. Penny found himself sitting up in bed. No. It wasn't an angel, exactly. It was . . . . His thoughts were so muddy and thick that it was hard to come up with the right word. A *monk*, maybe? Some holy-looking person in a coarse robe, at least. Eyes closed, hands clasped, the figure floated through the air, rooftops and cathedral spires far below. *Flying*. It was the flying part that made Mr. Penny assume, long ago, that it was a picture of an angel. Looking closely, though, there were no wings, or columns of light; nothing too angely, really. Just a scruffy old man serenely gliding over the cityscape.

★

The next day, Mr. Penny felt much better. He didn't realize it at first; had bounded out of bed and was half-way through making breakfast before it struck him. "Well, " he said, looking into the dog's buttony eyes, and flipping the bacon, "it looks like the soup worked after all. Sent those blue devils packing." Guy looked up at him, as happily as a dreary little sausage of a dog can. Mr. Penny gave him a piece of bacon, even though Mrs. Mickleson always cautioned him against this ("it bungs them up"). After downing his breakfast and cleaning the dishes, Mr. Penny threw on his favourite orange coat, and put Guy on his leash; then the two of them stepped out the door.

Mr. Penny had always thought of himself as a man of ideas. A lanky, shaky, and badly-made man, he'd have had little to recommend himself if it weren't for his imagination. Like the time—it was at a town meeting—when the Mayor had asked if anyone could think of a way of raising money for a new library, and Mr. Penny had suggested they could sell their houses. And when someone asked where they'd all live if they had no houses, Mr. Penny thought for a while, then said they could just build new ones. Everyone was speechless, after that.

Right now, he had another idea. It was the angel—or the monk, or whatever it was—that had given it to him. "I . . . am going . . . to *fly*," he said to himself, relishing every word like a mint under the tongue. Guy looked up at him, skeptically.

★

His first attempt was in Victoria Park. There were no big trees near Mr. Penny's building, but the park had plenty of them. He picked a tall one with red leaves and sturdy boughs, tied Guy to the trunk, and set about climbing it. After twelve feet or so, he stopped ("Good enough, for a first try"). But before he could jump—

"Now, what on earth are trying to do, there, Mr. Penny?" said a knobbly old woman, crossing her arms. It was Agnes Schmidt.

"Fly," said Mr. Penny, trying not to look at her. She was a nice woman. It's just that her skin was so withered, and her teeth so like a skeleton's teeth, that her appearance was—upsetting. Her arms and hands were so veined and spotted and prune-like that to watch her play the piano at church was to give up sleep till next Sunday. She never stopped moistening her lips, either. It was the sound of someone endlessly licking envelopes, or sucking gum, and Mr. Penny couldn't tolerate it.

"Young man, have you lost your head?" This was another old lady. It was sunny, so the park was filled with them.

"No," said Mr. Penny.

"Says he's gonna *fly*," explained Agnes to the other woman.

"Fly? Puh! Good Lord."

"Mr. Penny, I think you should come down here this instant."

"Why?"

"Because you'll break your bloody head, that's why," snapped the other woman.

Holding a branch with one hand to steady himself, Mr. Penny swung back his free arm.

"Don't you even think about it!"

He *did* think about it. And then, springing off the limb, with his arms outstretched . . .

A crackling, several gasps, and a thud.

"You damned crazy fool!"

"Oh! Are you all right?"

Mr. Penny got to his feet, untied Guy, and ran away.

★

At home, Mr. Penny sat in bed, wondering what had gone wrong. Now and then, he looked up at the picture of the flying man, then jotted something down in his notebook. *Could it have been the weather?* But that was silly. For a while, he thought maybe he wasn't holy enough to pull it off; the man was a monk after all. But no. He went to church every Sunday (*you can't go more often than that*); he was as holy as the next person. It had to be something else.

Mr. Penny got out of bed, and stood very close to the picture. He inspected every inch, top to bottom, side to side, looking for clues, some wonderful hidden something. And finally . . .

"Ah! I've got it, Guy. *See.*"

★

"Gold-coloured foil? Hmmm . . ."

The proprietor of Service Electric smoothed his moustache. His name was Reginald, but everyone in town called him Turkey (behind his back) because of his red complexion, and dangling neck fat. As for the shop, no one could really figure why the word "electric" appeared in its name, since hardly anything electrical was sold in it. Ditto "service," a rarity there, too. Mr. Penny was hoping the man wouldn't say, "Hmm . . . not at present. But I *just* ordered some," which was what he always said when he didn't have what people were looking for. Not wanting to look super-stitious or silly, Mr. Penny didn't *physically* cross his fingers—but he did so mentally, as best he could.

"Hmmm . . ." Turkey repeated, walking away. "There might be some in the back," vanishing behind a curtain that hung at the far end of the room.

As he waited, Mr. Penny looked around the shop. There were so many things crowded onto every shelf that it was a wonder Turkey wasn't able to summon forth anything a person cared to mention, presto, like some flabby, red magician. Pricey junk, most-ly: wind chimes, fake jewelry and such. There was even a dust-covered figurine of a superhero (the name escaped him) Mr. Penny had been fond of as a boy. He thought about buying it—*but it's way too much, really*—then did his best to think about other things. He remembered that, when he first came into the shop, Turkey had been flipping through a magazine that he quickly placed under the counter. Looking around carefully, first, to be sure the man wasn't coming, Mr. Penny stepped behind the counter, retrieved the magazine, opened it—and shut it, swiftly.

It was full of—well, *nude* people.

A shuffling, and a flapping of curtain. By the time Turkey made it back to the counter, gold foil in hand, Mr. Penny was smiling innocently on the other side of it.

★

It was exciting, spreading things out on the table exactly how one wanted them. Several times a week, Mr. Penny added to his scrapbooks—pictures of dogs and cats, mostly—and the setup for the present task was very much the same. The glue was at his left elbow, the scissors to his right, and in between, the gold foil, neatly smoothed out. He'd assumed the whole task would take a few minutes, at most, and he could try his creation out right away; but it took so long to get things how he wanted them it was already pretty dark, and any testing would have to wait until morning.

"What do you think?" he said to Guy, waving the finished product—a makeshift halo of cardboard and foil.

That night, Mr. Penny was so excited, he could hardly sleep. But—it's strange the way things work out—when morning came, he felt just *awful*. His alarm clock went off, as usual, at seven-thirty; but he let it ring down to silence without stirring. Ditto the telephone, even though he rarely received, and normally relished, any calls. Time passed (minutes or hours, he neither knew nor cared), and then—

A knock at the door.

"Mr. Penny? Are you there?"

It was Nurse Audrey. He could tell by her high nasal voice—like someone was squeezing her nostrils shut.

"Mr. Penny? I just want to talk."

That got him out of bed. Nurse Audrey—everyone has their oddities—generally only liked to talk to him after he'd been held down and poked with a needle.

"Are you alright?"

"Oh dear," he said aloud, wondering what on earth to do.

"I've heard some very distressing things, Mr. Penny. *Very* distressing."

As quickly as he could, he gathered up his clothes—no. There was no time for that. He put his slippers on, though, and Guy on his leash.

"Do you feel like hurting yourself?"

As quietly as he could, he opened the window, and removed the screen.

"Have you been taking your medication?"

"I almost forgot," he muttered, running to the kitchen, where he grabbed, not pills, but the halo.

"Step back from the door, sir," said a deep male voice.

Dog in arms, Mr. Penny climbed out the window.

★

Small towns are, for the most part, dull, uneventful places—or *safe* and *quiet*, as small-towners prefer to call them. That doesn't mean extraordinary things don't happen, on rare occasion—and when they do, they're relished all the more. A robbery barely makes page ten in a city; in a small town, it's worth a month of table talk, at the very least. So the sight of a man in pajamas racing through the streets, practically dragging a small dachshund behind him, hotly pursued by a nurse *and* two assistants was bound to arouse a little curiosity.

"Good Lord!" said—any number of people.

"Stop him! Stop him! Stop that man!" This was Nurse Audrey.

Being elderly, the bulk of the onlookers were much too frail to do anything as dramatic as that, but just frail enough to make their way after the other chasers in a kind of rapid straggle, eager to see what would happen next.

Mr. Penny, slowed down more than a little by Guy, still had a healthy head start. By the time he crossed the train tracks at the extreme south end of town, the mob had grown to nearly two dozen members; one would have thought the man was a celebrity, except that instead of crying for autographs, people murmured about "the bluffs"—a logical destination for any lunatic jumper, plunging as they did 200 feet down into the sea.

As it happened, Mr. Penny *was* headed for the bluffs; and it seemed likely he'd reach them without being stopped. There was a close call, when he stumbled on a clump of dirt ("Grab his legs," he'd heart Nurse Audrey say), but he managed to get up quickly and keep going. When he came very close to the precipice, he slowed to a stop, then turned about and faced his pursuers, who themselves stopped, afraid of his next move.

"It's alright, Mr. Penny," said Nurse Audrey, badly out of breath.

"What's alright?" said Mr. Penny.

"*Everything*," she replied. "Everything's just fine. Why don't you come away from that cliff? We can have a nice *talk*."

"No thank you," said Mr. Penny.

"He thinks he can fly, pour soul," said someone.

"I *can*," said Mr. Penny, irritated.

"Mmm hmm," said Nurse Audrey, solemn, nodding her head.

"You don't believe me," he said, glumly.

"You're a very *sick* man," she said.

Mr. Penny placed the halo on his head . . .

"Mr. Penny?" said the nurse, raising an eyebrow.

Picked up Guy . . .

"Mr. *Penny*?"

Turned about . . .

"Mr. Penny!"

And sprang over the cliff.

A medley of oaths, cries, declarations . . .

Then gasps, moans, and awed hush . . .

As Mr. Penny, serene, floated into the clouds.

The Visitor

Hello. Hello. Hi. I'm Anna. What's your name? I'm—that's okay. I'm just saying hello today. Just in . . . for a visit. Do you get many? Many visitors?

I'm from Wembley. Where you're from. Remember? Would you like to talk? It's alright. To talk. Or just to listen. If you like. Would you like just to listen? I'm from Wembley. Moore Street. The one by the river. The corner. Do you remember the brick house on the corner? I've lived there—twenty years, it must be. Twenty-one . . . twenty-two years. It seems longer. Do you find yourself that way? I find . . . it's so much longer. Than it is.

I knew your mother. I did. Pretty well, once. Quite well. Good friends. When we—were ten or twelve, I think, we—I'll always remember. Locked ourselves in . . . an upstairs closet. The door was the kind that. Snaps shut. Beat on the door and screamed and cried, sure we'd die in there, that we'd suffocate, no one would come looking. Of course, father rushed in, instantly. Laughed at us. Little idiots, called us. Laughing. I'll always remember.

Would you like some tea? I'm going to have a bit of tea. A spot of tea, as your mom would say. A spot of tea, and three lumps of sugar. Her usual. Too, too sweet for me. Not much of a tooth. A sweet tooth. More of a salt. Do you like salty things? Chips, pretzels? Popcorn? When I was—a little bit younger than before—five, maybe—I asked my Uncle Danny, Farmer Dan, what the blue things were in the pasture. Salt licks, he said. And I thought, that sounds appetizing, and I ran out onto the pasture when no one was looking and got down on my knees and licked one. Maybe that's . . . where I get it from.

Listen. I want to tell you something. If you don't want to be here. If there's somewhere else you can go. Someone who can help you, just tell me. It's alright to. If there's—anything I can do, believe me. You don't have to stay here. You only have to say. They need you to say, and if you're unhappy, maybe they can do something. You just have to speak up. It's alright.

You're upset. I've upset you. I'll—let's talk about something. Something else. They have a cat here, don't they? A—tortoise shell, is it? I think . . . you used to have a dog, didn't you? What kind was that? I think it was—what's the proper name—for a weenie dog? Dachshund. Inseparable. You two. A boy and his dog. A weenie dog. They were bred for—was it catching rabbits? Moles, or something. I think.

Let me know, if I'm boring you. Just shake your head, if you don't want to say. Won't hurt my feelings any. I can yap. I can talk too much. People tell me.

I can remember, when you—you must have been nine or something, ten. You went missing. Disappeared. Whole town in an—like an anthill. Two whole days, if I remember. Search parties. Police. And we found you, in the end—it was Janet Glass, the secretary, the school secretary—up a tree, the edge of town. Eating—apples, was it?

There—you're smiling. You're smiling, you remember. That's good. That's good. To see. Bet you were smiling in the tree, too, when they found you. A real tree nut, weren't you? A climber. Should've been the first place we looked, but. In an apple tree. Smiling.

Sorry about that. That silence. It's—well, it's not as if I've ever lacked things to say, but. When you're on the spot. You know.

Your mother. I am so sorry, we were all so sorry about your mother. A better situation, then, for you. But. You know, how life is.

Are you sure you don't want any tea?

I don't think—I know you would've been at the funeral. If you'd been able. I saw—your brothers. Do they ever come? I wonder. I'd heard—that they didn't. That was . . . part of it, part of the reason.

No tea? It isn't any trouble. I only have to press the button. And they'll come.

Let's see. Four o'clock. I have to—I still have to pick up Ashley. The airport. You remember my daughter? She was—no, she would've been the class—beneath you. Bit of a geek, those days. Braces. Beautiful girl, now. You should see her. Do I—no, I don't. No photograph. Sorry.

A nice garden. Out there. Do they—do you walk there, sometimes? Those . . . those are petunias. Roses. Gladiolas, I think. Beautiful. Lovely. Good to get out. Your room—well, it's stuffy, isn't it, it's snug. There isn't much light. It isn't healthy. I don't think.

No.

Well. It's been—I've enjoyed this. I really have. It makes a person feel good. To be helping. But those dishes don't do themselves, do they? I wish they did. A dish fairy. Easier, eh?

Sure you won't have any tea? Before I go? It's no trouble. Push a button. Or coffee? Unless you shouldn't. I've heard.

I talk too much.

Well. Do you mind? There. Everyone likes a hug, I find, needs one. From time to time. I'll see you. Another day, maybe. The budget's—once a year, only. But maybe. Another time. Glad I did this. Good to see you. Feels good. Remember. What I said.

Try to drink something. Some tea, or something.

Take care.

Try and take care.

Bye-bye.

Mr. Penny's Experience

When Mr. Penny died that night on the surgeon's table, it seemed to him as if the ceiling became wax, then papery, fog, then melted altogether. Loose strands of it remained, like arms of jellyfish, and brushed against him as he rose—or should have brushed him, only he felt nothing, despite being a notoriously ticklish man. He tried looking at his arms, but couldn't find them, and had the same trouble locating the rest of himself. *But there I am,* catching sight of a familiar-looking fellow on the table below, being thumped and prodded by a growing horde of white coats. He reached out, tried swimming downwards like a desperate frog, but with his limbs a good eight feet below, that hardly worked. Shouting proved equally ineffective. Nothing seemed to slow or stop his steady upward movement. This was a conundrum, and conundrums always gave Mr. Penny a migraine. So he turned his head (preferring to think he had one), and waited, as patiently as he could, to see what happened next. There were stars overhead now, and beneath him the frantic shouts and alarms grew softer every moment. He was glad to leave them behind. Soon there was nothing but darkness and stars all around.

Well this is different, he thought.

Mr. Penny had a sudden, strong impression of brightness behind him, not that he could see any actual trace of it. Still, to satisfy his curiosity, he turned around again, half-expecting a last far-off glimpse of the operating room. Instead, he saw the Earth itself, radiantly glowing, a marble.

A little flurry of panic. After all, he'd never been up this high before. But he adjusted quickly—a surprise even to himself. In no time moving bodilessly through space felt as natural as—(nothing had ever really felt natural to Mr. Penny. At least not in a very long time).

Before he really had time to admire the beauty of the planet, it had shrunk to a star-sized dot. This was, of course, a major disappointment. Mr. Penny didn't know when he'd have the opportunity to view it from such a height again, and worried it was one of those "once in a lifetime" things people were always talking about. *I should have brought my camera.* As he moved along, the dot vanishing altogether, the likelihood that it *was* a once in a lifetime thing seemed strong. *It was a nice place*, he thought, trying to console himself, *but I've seen enough of it.*

The loneliness, the strange newness of the circumstances would have troubled most people, but Mr. Penny didn't really mind. He was by nature a solitary man, a retiring one, and when he did venture out, found the world pretty baffling in general. Besides, there were so many interesting things to look at. There were stars, millions of them, but he couldn't find any of the constellations he liked. For a while he wished he had his telescope; though after passing right through one star (he liked to think it prickled), Mr. Penny realized he was as close to the universe as anyone could care to be.

There seemed to be no end of wonders. Flying rocks. Bursts of light. Clouds of all hues and sizes. The first time Mr. Penny approached one of these clouds (it was purple), he grew unbearably excited, and couldn't wait to see what it would be like in the midst of all that colour. The closer he came, though, the further away the substance of the cloud seemed to be, until, to his disappointment, it thinned out and faded into nothing. *A lot like walking into fog*, he thought. *You never really get to it.* Still, Mr. Penny enjoyed traveling through these elusive mists; liked going through the pink ones best of all, and imagined the whole thing was more fun that it really was. More than once he encountered burning ice, which he wouldn't have believed unless he'd seen it, and had the good fortune to catch a glimpse an outrageously big planet suddenly go flat as a cat's whisker, then vanish altogether. Though he'd seen that with his own eyes, he *still* couldn't believe it.

There were, of course, long stretches where there was nothing in particular to look at. To pass the time during these periods,

Mr. Penny tried counting stars. But they vanished and reappeared so quickly that the whole thing was just too frustrating. Adding to the frustration was the fact that the speed at which he traveled never stayed the same for long. At times he went so fast that the stars around him went from streaks to long dotted lines to nothing at all, just hurtling darkness, and he missed lots of good stuff. At other times, he barely seemed to go at all, which was fine if there was something to look at, but . . .

Just when he was starting to get bored, Mr. Penny noticed something that, even under the circumstances, he found strange.

At first, it looked like any of the small specks of light he'd been zipping past, for how long he wasn't sure. As he came closer, though, slowing every moment, he couldn't help but notice that *this* speck had a unique quality. It appeared to be, hovering in the middle of space no less, a nicely furnished living room without a roof (*like at a play*, thought Mr. Penny). From the main room lolled a long red-carpeted hallway, curving downwards where it ended. In the middle of the room was a low table, complete with silver tea service and a basket of what appeared to be scones. Around the table were a dozen or so high-backed wooden chairs, painted black. All of them were unoccupied but one, which bore the weight of a plump, sweet-looking elderly woman.

Alighting on the carpet, very close to the sloping curve, Mr. Penny was glad to see that, first of all, he had his body back, and everything was where it ought to be. He was also relieved that the carpet bore his weight as well as any solid floor, and he didn't go falling down into space.

He wasn't sure what to do next, so he looked around, and got to noticing things. It was a very nice hallway; probably the nicest he'd ever been in. Lining the walls were gold-framed paintings of men and women, some in old-fashioned clothes, some in modern ones. But they were all painted in the same fancy way, *and probably by the same person*, thought Mr. Penny. The temperature of the hall was just right. Mr. Penny had always found that most people's houses were far too cold. And though he couldn't find any source of light—there was no ceiling, after all, and nothing on the walls—the whole place was well lit, and as cheerful as he could have wished it.

From his vantage at the end of the hallway, Mr. Penny could see only a small portion of the room to which it lead—essentially, the back of one of the chairs, and above that the head of the woman seated at the opposite end of the table. She smiled in silence. Mr. Penny took a few nervous steps forward. It was nice, after such a long journey, to finally have some company, *and she looks pleasant enough*. Still, he was skeptical. From experience, he'd learned that an awful lot of women who look pleasant and have nice painted-on smiles will nonetheless whop you with a purse if you get an inch too close. *This one doesn't seem to have a purse, thankfully*. On her teacup fingers—I mean, the ones she was holding her teacup with—were several large, glittering rings. With her free hand, she toyed with a string of—*not pearls, but white beads*. Her tightly curled hair was almost certainly dyed (red). She wore a bit too much make-up.

"Mr. Penny," she said, refilling her cup. "I've been expecting you."

"*Me?*" He could hardly believe it.

"Tea?"

"Free," said Mr. Penny, thinking it was a rhyming game.

"Oh, it won't cost you a dime," said the woman. "Take a seat." He did—the one furthest from her, but nearest to the scones—looking about nervously as she filled his cup.

He was a bit reluctant to drink it. She was a stranger, after all. Though she was old, and most old people, Mr. Penny had found, are kind, he knew it was never a good idea to trust just anyone. But she downed the stuff herself without any apparent discomfort, and looked harmless enough. Besides, he didn't want to upset her. So he took a small mouthful, and was pleased to find that it tasted like plain old black China tea. He might have wondered where on earth she got it from—but didn't.

"Scone?" she asked.

Being partial to scones, he didn't hesitate to take one.

"No butter, I'm afraid," noticing how he looked about the table forlornly. "A little hard to come by in these parts."

"That's alright," he said, trying not to sound disappointed.

"How was the journey down?"

It had seemed more like a journey *up* to him, though all he said was, "Fine, thanks." It was his favourite expression, and usually all he had to say to anyone. The same people, he'd noticed, who would stop him in the street to say "And how are *you*?" talked to other people about all kinds of things—movies, weddings, politics. But with him, strangely, they never wanted to know anything more than how he *was*. It was a conundrum.

"If you have any questions," said the woman, after a long pause, "don't hesitate to ask."

"Umm . . ." Mr. Penny thought for a while. It's not that there weren't a million things he wanted to ask or could have asked. It's just that he wasn't very good at conversations, especially when the other person was looking you right in the eye. The newness of the place didn't help, either. So he timidly picked at the scone, and looked around the room.

Like the hall, it had an elegant, expensive look. There were plenty of tall, potted plants, and each of the several shelves and stands which stood in the corners had a doily and at least one glass curio on it. Though the room was bright—even brighter that the hall—he looked in vain for a lamp or a candle or even a switch. There were three doors: one just behind the woman's chair, and one each on the walls to her left and right. Just over her shoulder was a painting of—*well, it has to be her*, thought Mr. Penny. *When she was younger.* The painted figure reclined against a piano, smiling. And there was another painting, too.

"Is that *me*?" asked Mr. Penny, astounded. He looked so young—about nineteen or twenty—that he barely recognized himself. His picture-self sported a trim moustache *(I can never get it even anymore)* and the same orange coat he'd worn to the hospital, only brand new-looking instead of ratty. There was a briefcase in his hand. Suddenly, he didn't want to look at the picture anymore.

"You've had a very long trip," said the woman. "You must be tired."

Mr. Penny nodded. He suddenly was.

"Perhaps you'd like to go to your room?"

He nodded again, and said, "Yes, thank you. But—I'm afraid it's a long way off by now."

She smiled. "I wasn't talking about your *old* room."

"Oh," said Mr. Penny, slouching a little.

"I was talking about the *new* one."

"New?" said Mr. Penny, sitting upright.

"Of course. I should think you had the old one long enough. Ten years, was it? Dismal little place, especially after your mother died. Lonesome, too, I'll bet?"

A comet passed overhead, leaving behind a dusty trail that settled over the room. The woman quickly put her hand over her teacup, and Mr. Penny followed suit.

"It was lonely, yeah," he said. "But Mrs. Mickleson was just next door. She made very good scones. These ones are good, too," he added quickly, not wanting to offend her.

"No doubt, no doubt," she said, taking another big gulp. And after a while, "There's a time for everything, Mr. Penny, and I'd say it's high time for a *change*." She refilled her cup. "What do you say?"

He was about to blurt out "Yes, please," when the thought struck him that the new room might be more cramped and cold than the last one, so it wouldn't be a good trade after all. A person has to be careful. The new room could even have a rodent in it. Mr. Penny couldn't tolerate rodents. It's true that they're *sort of* cute when you see them in pet shops, or pictures in books, but when they're skittering up your pant leg, well, it's quite another matter. Mr. Penny's old room had rodents in it when he first moved in. That was before he had a dog. It was just awful.

"What *kind* of room," he asked, cautiously.

"It's a lovely room, really," refilling her teacup. The woman went on in short bursts between sips, "Four-post bed. Toilet with shower. Sink and stove in perfect condition. A window on each wall. A few cracks on the linoleum—but nothing's perfect, eh, Mr. Penny? Excellent view of the stars, of course."

"But what's it per month?" he asked, suddenly skeptical, knowing he only got so much, and the room sounded too good to be true.

"No charge," said the woman, finishing off the cup. "And you can stay as long as you like."

Mr. Penny was in awe. "Are you God?" he asked, finally.

The woman flushed. "Bless you, dear. I'm just the old house-keeper."

"Oh." Mr. Penny looked admiringly at the silver tea service, the paintings, the furniture. "Am *I* God?" he ventured.

The woman only smiled.

"Some more tea, Mr. Penny?" she asked.

Mr. Penny thought carefully, then answered, "Yes."

NOTES AND SALUTATIONS

"Von Claire and the Tiger" first appeared in *Short Story America*, and subsequently in the *Short Story America Anthology*. It was awarded the 2007 John Kenneth Galbraith Literary Award (Canada), and nominated for a Pushcart (2010).

"God's Autobio" first appeared in *Lunch Hour Stories*, and subsequently in both *Short Story America*, and the *Short Story America Anthology*.

"The Splendid New Crack" first appeared in *New York Tyrant*.

"Anna" was first podcast by *Bound Off*.

"Chimpanions" first appeared in *The Labletter*.

Both "Etiquette" and "Mr. Penny's Experiment" first appeared in *Transition*.

A truncated version of "Mr. Penny's Experience" (as "The Expedition") was one of the winners of the 2008–2009 Commonwealth Short Story Competition. It first appeared on the CD *Commonwealth Short Stories 2008–2009*, and was subsequently broadcast on radio programs worldwide, including CBC Radio's SoundXchange.

"The Man With the Ridiculously Huge Coupon" first appeared in *SmokeLong Quarterly*.

"Tonight" first appeared in *Underground Voices*.

Many thanks to the editors/producers/readers/organizers/hosts of the above, especially Tim Johnston, Jenny Phillips, Ted Dyck, Lynn Hill, Giancarlo DiTrapano, Sarah Elizabeth Marrs, Robert Kotchen, Ann Rushton, Kelly Shriver, Joanne Skidmore, Jim Tucker, and Barbara Barnes.

Many thanks to my publisher, Sidney Shapiro, and everyone at Now Or Never.

Many thanks to my "groupies," who first listened to (and improved) many of the stories: Jo-Anne Grayson, Bette Ramshaw, Heather Roske, and Betty Terschuur.

Many thanks, as well, to Ashley. Having at least one vocally supportive family member is always helpful.